Can't Beat the Heart of a Carolina Girl

Allyson Kennedy

Disclaimer

This is a work of fiction. Names, characters, businesses, places, events and incidents are either the products of the author's imagination or used in a fictitious manner. Any resemblance to actual persons, living or dead, or actual events is purely coincidental.

Can't Beat the Heart of a Carolina Girl

ISBN-10: 1543176712
ISBN-13: 978-1543176711

Dedication

This is for all the girls who deem themselves as shy, awkward, and feel as if they don't have what it takes to make something of themselves one day. You can, and you will, and it will be amazing.

Chapter One

Does the quality of a yearbook picture have the power to predict how a school year will turn out? If so, I've discovered why I've hated my past three years at Grahamwood Junior High. Scattered on my bedroom floor, my yearbooks create a time machine, blasting me back to times I wish I could forget. Any chance of a smile disintegrates as I stumble across my sixth grade photograph. Each yearbook picture I've taken acts as a stepping stone to the land of dorkdom since that horrid year. If it wasn't for my cousin Grace's lack of cosmetology skills, my flowing locks of golden blonde hair would still be intact. Suffice it to say that a mangled haircut was the last element needed to ensure three years of torture.

The gawks I received the first week back to school made me want to hide away like Quasimodo forever. My classmates were relentless, mocking my appearance and shunning me from all cliques. If it wasn't the haircut that turned them away, it was my braces and the rubber bands I had to wear with them. Further dwindling my confidence, I'm far from my crush's radar, let alone his league. But I can't blame him for chasing after the goddesses that walk the halls of Linwood Whaley High instead of me. Brett Harvey is my next-door neighbor, and I've known him my entire life, though he's so caught up in other things to ever notice his awkward little admirer over the fence. Aside from that, he's two years older than me, the quarterback on the Linwood Whaley High School football team, and a goldmine of good looks. An infatuation going on seven years, which has yet to garner any results, I'm convinced that ever capturing his interest will be a futile feat.

To make matters worse, middle school was a terror trap in which I survived utterly alone. During a random fourth-grade recess, I learned that my best friend had moved away. When my classmates broke off into different cliques, I was left isolated, wondering of Lexie's whereabouts. Once, on a confident whim, I approached the group of popular girls in an attempt to broaden my circle. Their ringleader took one glance at my new Aeropostale T-shirt and whispered to her clones, "Yeah, Aero's definitely out now." So, deem me a loner if you want; it's nothing I haven't heard.

Offensive or not, I'm through with falling victim to slanderous words. I've been insulted to the point I've grown a thick skin, shielding my heart from their meaningless comments. Yet this year, I plan to make my rebirth in the world as a girl people will love and respect.

This seemingly far-fetched goal became possible by subjecting my appearance to a major overhaul. Since the traumatic haircut, I've allowed my hair to grow into longer, luscious blonde strands. Only licensed stylists have permission to make any necessary changes (no offense, Grace). Having my braces removed in July became the last step of resigning from my dork-princess days. Needless to say, I no longer flinch when I catch sight of my reflection.

Closing the book, an epiphany arises, knowing that those days of torture will now be few and far between. I will no longer remain stepped on. I will not back down from fear. From this moment, I vow to take a bold leap into my new territory tomorrow at 8:00 a.m.: Linwood Whaley High School.

⌘

My first morning at Linwood Whaley High begins by following the droves of students to the main building from the drop-off area. The moment I walk through the front double doors, my stomach churns, as if urging my morning Poptart to make a reappearance. Though the maroon and charcoal walls decorated with past Arrowhead achievements evoke a welcoming atmosphere, the scowls on the upperclassmen do not. Despite my aspirations, my gaze remains glued to the glowing waxed floors as I attempt to navigate my way to homeroom.

Upon locating Room 4, I wait for the homeroom bell to ring, anxious in all aspects. An eternity seems to pass before other people start to settle into the seats around me. My luck, the first person I recognize from middle school is the inglorious Hailey Carson. My stomach performs a triple-flip as

I imagine the horrors I will be facing for the rest of this semester. The fact that she offers a pitying glance at her cohorts as they walk by my desk confirms my fears.

Hailey, the bane of my existence since the fifth grade, is the original mastermind behind the rude comments made about my appearance. Holding the top-ranked spot on the list of people I detest most, she's easily a ten on the obnoxious meter. But, being that her parents spoil her to the core, enable her shopping habits, and take up for her narcissistic ways, she's merely a product of her environment, aka her world.

As if *one* dollar-diva isn't enough, her two evil minions, Tiffany and Nichole, follow her in suit. "Oh great, best day ever," I mumble to myself. Resting my head on the desk, I'm already praying for this semester to be as short-lived as summer vacation.

A sigh of relief escapes me as Mrs. Wilson makes her way into the classroom. The teachers at Grahamwood Junior High told us that she is one of the nicest staff members, though her teaching expertise is limited to electives like Home Economics. Mrs. Wilson passes out student schedules, and I'm elated to find that I have English this semester. Writing poetry has served as my escape since I picked up the hobby in seventh grade, and Language Arts was my best subject in middle school. Maybe there'll be some hope for this year, after all.

Glancing back at my schedule, my hope falters when I notice that I've been sentenced to Earth Science for third period. Reminiscing back to junior high, flashbacks of suffering through labs and lectures fill me with dread. Being that I passed the class with a C in seventh grade (though I graduated at the top of my class) makes my stomach lurch more.

After Mrs. Wilson finishes passing out schedules, she reads aloud the school rules from the student handbook. Figuring that listening will be a waste of time since I'm not a trouble-making student anyway, I opt to write a poem on the back of my schedule:

Watch me defy gravity

With every step I take.

I'll walk around air-free

At last carefree

Released of past mistakes.

I will not remain restrained.

I will not be cast into darkness.

I will not stand to be pushed down,

Because I'm marching on my own ground.

These dreams are my turf,

My destiny is my guide.

You will not control me this time.

Can't Beat the Heart of a Carolina Girl

No matter how hard you try,

I will discover my own way.

I will do as I say,

I will make something of myself.

Better than I was

Captive on the dusty shelf.

I'm free. I'm me.

At last, defying gravity.

As I've mentioned, I have been writing a lot of poems within the last year and a half, collecting them in a notebook stored beneath my bed. Momma read one of them once and told me that it was amazing. Deep down I hope it is, but still, she is my mother, and we all know how they love to tell us our creations are pure genius.

Soon the bell rings, dismissing us from homeroom. As I'm stuffing my schedule and handbook into my bookbag, Hailey prances up behind me, looking for a target. "Isn't that like a loner to sit by herself and write all the time? Who needs a guy in their life when you have... hmm? What exactly do you have, Riley?"

Rolling my eyes, I scurry out of the classroom in silence. There's no need to defend myself, for every time I've tried doing that in the past, I end up embarrassing myself more. My mind flits back to the sixth grade when I caught her bullying a younger kid that attends the same church as me. Quick to jump to his defense, I took the chance to stand up to Hailey for all the havoc she has wreaked. Instead of backing down, she shifted her ridicule to me, bringing to light every flaw that I was already aware of in myself. So yeah, I have my reasons.

Hmm, first period. Where is that again? To ease my confusion, I try to pull my schedule back out of my bookbag. Tugging and struggling with all my might, the stupid thing refuses to budge, being that it got caught in the zipper. Seconds later, it becomes unstuck, causing the whole thing to unzip. Spilling out of the bag, my notebooks scatter on the floor around me. I thank God for a second that I'm so invisible that no one saw that happen. Yet, as I bend down to pick up my belongings, I hear a voice a little down the hall.

"Hey, need some help?"

Looking up with an embarrassed semblance, I'm shocked to see Brett coming down the hall toward me. He walks past his friend Sawyer, calling over his shoulder that he'll catch up with him at lunch. For a second, I debate if he's actually coming toward me, or if this is yet another fake-out I'll be mortified over for years to come. Instead, as he steps closer he offers a wave, and I'm caught up in the fact that he looks even better with a tan. With the apples of my cheeks tinting pink at his words, I strain for the nerve to reply, "Yeah, thanks!"

He squats, collecting a binder and a couple spiral notebooks. As you can tell, I'm that nerd who comes fully prepared on the first day of school. Rearranging them by size, he hands them back to me, revealing a soft smile. Awestruck at the fact that he approached me, I can't help but become distracted by his eyes. A majestic dark brown, it's as if they form a black hole in which I can't escape from—a portal that allows me to look straight into his heart, into a future I'm convinced I'll one day be a part of.

"Riley?" Brett whispers, producing a wary look. I must have been staring too long. Then again, I've never been able to be inconspicuous about these things.

"Oh, sorry!" I mumble, jolting back into a standing position when I realize I'm still on the ground. "Thanks again, Brett!"

I turn to walk off, but a question reels me back in. "So, what class do you have for first period?"

Pivoting around, I take another gander at my schedule, my hand shaking. "Looks like Career Management." I force a smile, attempting to overshadow my nerves.

"Cool, I have Accounting. It's right down the hall. Do you wanna walk together?"

You have no clue how much of a major breakthrough this is for me, being that this is the first time Brett has talked to me outside of our neighborhood. "Sure," I reply, though hesitant, as we take off to the school's business and technology building out back.

Our conversation involves what we did over the summer, my heart pounding harder with every step we take. Though I still feel as if I'm making a meager dent in the shell I oh-so-desperately want to escape from, there's a hint of confidence in my voice. Every past attempt at talking to him has resulted in me either chickening out or saying something mortifying. However, now that he has approached me, this might have the potential to go somewhere.

We reach our classroom doors, departing to go our separate ways. Watching him wave goodbye to me, I decide that this year may possibly surpass my expectations.

Chapter Two

Career Management passed faster than expected, though my mind was fogged over after I was escorted to class by a certain junior hottie. The same thing happened in second period. I can't shake the fact that he even talked to me when most of the time he acts as if he doesn't know me. Still, it occurs to me that he might want to now.

Currently, I'm making my way to my third period class, located on the second floor of the main school building. Ah, Earth Science. My nose wrinkles at the thought of what I may have to suffer through this semester, what with my limited interest and knowledge of all things scientific.

Cracking open the door to the classroom, the chatter of students leaks into the hallway. Glancing at the faces as I search for an open seat, I don't know anyone and no one appears as if they are interested in getting to know me, so I sit down toward the back of the room and try not to get noticed.

Minutes later, a bunch of jocks from my old school walk in. *Oh no*, I judge, *here's to another semester of having to sit through class overhearing their perverted conversations.* They head past me to the rear of the room, as they want to be concealed from the teacher whenever class starts.

Surprising me, one pats my desk and comments, "Hey, Riley." Looking up, I recognize him as Jesse, one of the nicer guys of the group. As I say hi back, he smiles down at me, and follows his pack of friends.

I can hear them talking, since they're always the loudest in a crowded room. At least I'm not eavesdropping. Oh well, so maybe I am, but I'm bored out of my mind. It's not like I can stop them anyway, so it peaks my interest to listen in on their conversation.

"Dude, are you sure that was Riley?" one of them named Jeremy asks.

"Yeah, pretty sure. Why?"

"She sure didn't look like that the last time I saw her. She had that jacked up hair that made her look like those twins from *The Suite Life of Zack and Cody,* and those freaky robot braces! How the heck did she go from that to hot overnight?"

My nosy nature comes to a halt, my eyes widening in bewilderment at Jeremy's admittance. Yeah, I had a little makeover session going on prior to the new school year, but it never occurred to me that I would reap any special attention from it. I've recently started wearing makeup, so that could have helped, though my basic routine consists of foundation and a bit of mascara. Whatever I've done, I guess it's working if Jeremy, the crown jewel of our middle school, thinks I'm hot.

Can't Beat the Heart of a Carolina Girl

Seconds before the late bell chimes, my cousin Trent rushes in. Tottering over strewn bookbags, he chooses to sit at the empty desk next to me. Trent didn't go to Grahamwood like me; he attended Corley Creek Middle School, where his dad works as a gym teacher. Because Linwood Whaley High is a combination of the two schools—Grahamwood and Corley Creek—I now have the interesting opportunity to be in class with one of my favorite cousins.

"Awesomeness, you have this class too?" he greets, waving in my face like the goofball he is. "Yes! Now I can copy off someone other than Carter!"

"Trent, you're not copying my work! I feel sorry for the poor sap, whoever he is, for having to deal with you all the time," I retort, trying to keep a straight face.

"Hey now, Carter's the man! He's my best friend, Riles. In fact, you two act a lot alike." Plopping down in his seat, he cracks his knuckles as if he's about to cut me a deal. "I'll even introduce you to him if you want? He's single," Trent allures, wiggling his eyebrows for effect.

Before I can object, our teacher barges in, balancing a Styrofoam cup of coffee and a brown bag from Hardee's on top of his teaching supplies. "Hello, my name is Charles Donoghue. I'll be your teacher this semester." He then relays that he earned a teaching degree in New Jersey before moving to North Carolina.

"Northerner in redneck central; this should be good," I whisper to Trent, after noticing two guys a couple rows over from us making fun of Mr. Donoghue's accent.

"Now I don't know any of you, and many of you don't know one another, but I believe I have a method to mend that barrier. Each of you may come to the front of the class and tell us something interesting about yourself. Starting with you."

Naturally, he ends up pointing at me. I don't know why on Earth he pointed at me, but he did. I swallow my nerves as I reluctantly make my way to the front of the classroom. Though I wouldn't classify myself as shy, public speaking has freaked me out as long as I can remember, dating back to my first Christmas play at church where I went on stage and immediately froze stiff. Fast-forward to age fourteen, and nothing has changed. Everyone staring at me with what feels like judgmental gawks is making it much worse.

"Well, what's your name?" Mr. Donoghue tries to sound encouraging, but it isn't helping in the slightest.

"Riley Houston," I mutter, audible enough for the first row to hear. If they were dogs, that is.

"Go on, please."

"I'm from Grahamwood, and I like to write poems." An awkward silence settles throughout the classroom; the same guys who were mocking our teacher share a look of repulsion at the mention of my hobby. Mr. Donoghue offers a sympathetic smile, allowing me to return to my seat. I'm convinced that everyone will now consider me the class freak, my former title. No one besides me at Grahamwood liked to write, so why would any of them?

Once I've melted back into my seat, desperate to become invisible, Mr. Donoghue asks for more testimonials. I'm relieved that Trent volunteers to go up after me and accidentally farts on the way back. I guess awkwardness runs in the family.

When the little meet and greet session is over, Mr. Donoghue allows us to talk among ourselves. Trent retreats to go find Carter for me, being that he's supposedly somewhere in this class amongst the other thirty students. The two remain MIA for a few minutes because Jesse and Jeremy are playing around with a football in the back of the room, causing Trent to have to dodge the ball every five seconds.

While awaiting his return, a lilac fingernail taps my shoulder. Turning around, a girl with strawberry blonde hair is waving at me. I can't recall who she is based on our introductions, but I wave back anyway.

"Hi, I'm Taylor! I heard you say that you like to write, which is a rarity around here. I've been writing this story about a girl who lives in the Appalachians. Could you read it and tell me what you think?"

She starts to pass over a composition book to me, when Trent runs back to my desk, whispering in an ecstatic squeak, "I found him!"

Smiling, I roll my eyes. "Okay, Trent. Simmer down."

Taylor shakes her head. "You'll have to excuse him. He's a tad hyper if you haven't already noticed. We went to Corley Creek together."

"Oh, I'm used to it." I laugh. "He's my cousin. I know how weird he is."

This elicits a snort from Taylor, yet Trent fails to accept my humor. "Yeah Riley, go ahead, be mean! I don't have to introduce you to Carter, you know!"

"Funny, because I don't remember asking for that favor. You're the one that keeps going on about the fact that he's single and that I need to meet him," I argue.

"Alright, that's it!" He smirks back at me, his freckles making him appear younger than he is. "Hey Carter, come here!"

A guy seated four or five rows away stands to join our conversation, leaning against Trent's desk due to the lack of available chairs. He appears to be a nice guy, and kind of cute. Okay, so that may be an understatement. Short brown hair reaches the top of his ears, and the brightest ice blue eyes look down on me. They're almost as stunning as Brett's, though his are brown. Carter's face turns red as he meets my gaze, a definite sign of a shy guy. How on earth does he deal with Trent all the time?

"Riley, this is my best friend, Carter. Carter, this is Riley, my cousin." Trent gestures, sinking back into his chair, a grin the size of a crescent moon plastered on his face.

"Hey Riley. Trent's told me so much about you over the years. You seem pretty cool based on what he's said," Carter admits, his country accent drawling as low as my introduction minutes ago.

His nervous demeanor lessens as I return, "Oh, thanks! You seem nice, too." I poke Trent's arm. "As long as you promise not to help this one cheat through class. He's already tried to weasel me into it."

Carter allows a soft laugh to escape, eyeing his friend in a skeptical manner. "That's easier said than done. This guy's the reigning king of sneaky tactics, but I'm sure you already know that." I smile at his wit, and of course, the bell rings.

As we're gathering our belongings, Carter ventures back to retrieve his bookbag from across the room. Once he's out of earshot, I offer an apology to my cousin. "Alright Trent, so I may have underestimated you. Carter seems pretty decent. Who knows, I may owe you for this one day."

Trent, cocky as ever, returns, "Heck yeah, I knew you'd understand, Riles! Now I have every right to copy your work. See, everyone wins!"

Rolling my eyes at his comment, I force my way out of the classroom before him. Even if he has done one nice thing for me, I still can't overlook the fact that he'll take advantage of me every chance he gets.

Chapter Three

Lunch serves as the most frightening part of my first day experience, as I imagined. Walking into the cafeteria after third period, it seems as if a sea of a million souls is crowded into the two serving lines. The single lesson I learn on the first day of school is that "third lunch" is a term interchangeable with "the table scraps left from feeding time at the water hole".

Waiting in the lunch line for thirteen minutes results in obtaining a soggy BBQ rib sandwich that resembles something my neighbor's Cocker Spaniel produces in Momma's flower garden nearly twice a week. So much for healthy school food.

Finding a seat in the midst of the chaos proves to be the most difficult task. Everywhere I look, kids appear hateful, while others are downright scary. I opt to sit in an empty seat beside a trash can, when a golden halo appears on a table where some kids from Grahamwood are gathered. I've never spoken to them all that much, but at this point my choices are fleeting.

Aiming to keep a positive outlook, I settle down into the last available seat. Some of them glance up for half a millisecond, but the majority fails to notice. Truth be told, I consider this rather disturbing, as a convict could have done the same thing and no one would have been fazed. Taking a bite into my sandwich, I prefer to keep to myself, blocking out

18

the X-rated conversations going on around me. Finding another table will become my top priority tomorrow. Ignoring them to the best of my ability, I finish scarfing down the rest of my food right before the bell for fourth period rings. English, finally! I hurry from the crowded lunchroom, tossing my trash in the bin near the double doors, excited for my last class of the day.

Entering Room 12 with a confident smile, I've assured myself that Honors English will be a breeze. Being the first to arrive, I choose a desk in the middle of the classroom. Within a couple minutes, Taylor emerges through the doorway. Maybe having a writing friend isn't an impossible dream.

The bell signals the class to begin, failing to overshadow the sound of the teacher's heels as she steps into the classroom. Standing at six feet tall, Mrs. Griffin immediately demands the attention of the class. Donning long graying hair, she has an air of professionalism about her that suggests she's been teaching for no less than a couple decades.

The first words out of her mouth notify us that we are expected to read six novels this semester. Two will be individual book reports, while the other four are required readings that will make up test material. This mention scares the snot out of me as reading has never been a beloved pastime of mine, despite my love for poetry. I'm also a world-renowned procrastinator, so I figure that this announcement is comparable to a murder attempt on the class, being that most members of the freshman class are more or less the same way.

Can't Beat the Heart of a Carolina Girl

Adding to my dimming opinion of this class, Mrs. Griffin announces that we'll have homework tonight. And so my last speck of hope deteriorates. Thankfully, the assignment is to write a poem. Smiling to myself, I'm quick to thank God for this blessing. If I can't write a new poem by tomorrow, I'll turn in one of my older ones. There's no way she can turn this into a negative thing for me.

There is no way, until she mentions that we are required to memorize our poems and recite them to the class tomorrow. It was hard enough for me last period to introduce myself! Now I'm expected to express my thoughts and feelings aloud to the public's ears, without having the knowledge if they will like the darn thing in the first place.

Though I entered the class full of optimism with a smile to show it, I leave with a pitiful frown, disheartened after the final dismissal bell rings. A morose walk to the school's front lawn fails to ease my frustration. Checking the time on my cell phone, I calculate the minutes it'll take for Momma to arrive. She has to pick my younger sister up from elementary school, so I wait outside for what seems like an eternity.

Over the glacial passage of time, I catch sight of Brett leaving the student parking lot in his Chevy Silverado. His parents aren't what I would consider well-off, yet they provide top-of-the-line gifts for him anyway. At times, I empathize for his younger siblings, who are often overlooked since he's the oldest. My sister, Remy, has tried to warn me that he is too self-centered to take notice in someone like me—as she's friends with his little brother, Ben—but today has proved her judgment wrong. Besides, over the past fourteen years, my intuition has had a ninety-four percent accuracy rate.

No less than fifteen minutes later, Momma's Pacifica speeds into the school's drop-off and pick-up driveway. I can't manage to buckle my seat belt before she ambushes me with questions about my first day as a freshman. At first, I don't know where to start, for my day has had many ups and downs. Nevertheless, the highlight of my day is still Brett's act of hallway chivalry, so I rehash that story first.

And within the blink of an eye, my first day of high school is over. I'm still somewhat shocked that I powered through without having an anxiety attack. Still, I'm aware that there will be many more trials and errors to face in the year to come; however, I have faith that God will make this one to remember.

⌘

Arriving back home at three-thirty, I immediately climb the stairs to my room to locate my poetry notebook. Hopefully I'll come across one good enough to submit for my English homework. Searching amidst the dozen or so notebooks stashed under my bed, it takes me a while to locate the one I'm looking for. I haven't written a poem in a while minus the one I chicken-scratched today in homeroom, so this one, in particular, may be difficult to locate.

Rummaging through them, I seize the purple covered notebook, decorated with a thin layer of dust. Skimming through the numerous pieces, I set out on an intensive search for the perfect one. Poems that pertain to my personal life are out of the question, yet I fear to present one that gives off a distant vibe. I've managed to kill half an hour by rereading them when I come across one I wrote over the summer that has since become one of my favorites. Entitled "Blue Eyes", it's a short piece I wrote centered on the beautiful peepers of a certain Mr. Harvey. The title is a misnomer, since Brett has brown eyes, but I figured changing the color would conceal my crush's identity if anyone were to ever wonder who the subject of the poem is. Adding a little anonymity, if you catch my drift, despite the fact that no one besides me even knows this poem exists.

Reading back over "Blue Eyes" a couple times convinces me that it will be the perfect piece to recite in English tomorrow, though the thought crosses my mind that it would be even better if Brett were in the class to hear it. The fact that he's two grades ahead of me and already has his license often makes me uneasy, based on the notion that he's most likely interested in a girl of the same caliber, one with more experience than my nonexistent dating resume currently holds.

Taking the time to memorize the poem, I'm satisfied with my ability to recall every word within ten minutes.

Uttering a quick prayer, I ask God for enough courage to avoid freaking out when it's my turn to recite.

Returning the notebook to its proper place, my diary catches my eye, beckoning for information about my first day at Linwood Whaley High. My encounter with Brett takes up most of the page, recounting every precious detail. However, when I mention third period and Carter comes to mind, my thought process hits a wall. I don't know why I'm transfixed on what a cute personality he seems to have, and that he admitted I was cool (nervously, no less!). An involuntary smile spreads upon my lips, though at the realization I'm taken aback and kick my diary back under the bed.

Chapter Four

Day 2 at Linwood Whaley High begins as a direct result of a Ctrl-v of yesterday's proceedings. Nichole and Tiffany start rumors about some guy named Joel in our homeroom, while I sit back and attempt to ignore them. My thoughts wander to Brett, jolting back to the fact that he doesn't have a girlfriend. I relish the thought, knowing that he had been the one helping me in the hall.

The first period bell notifies us to get going, causing me to stuff the mandatory student information sheets into my bookbag. Trying to remain calm, I exit into the hallway, hoping I'll see Brett on the way like I had yesterday. Among the students chatting and hustling to get to class, there's no sign of him, but someone else catches my eye... Carter. From across the hall, we make eye contact, causing a half-smile to play across his lips. I swear he's about to make his way toward me.

I raise my hand to wave at him, to find myself being interjected by none other than Mr. Harvey himself.

"Hey Riley, want to walk with me again today? The freshmen are prone to get lost the first few days, and I don't want you to be late on my account." He laughs, blocking my view of Carter.

24

Shoving my hand into my jacket pocket, I'm quick to reply, "Yeah, sounds great!" Glancing back over my shoulder at Carter as we're leaving, I watch him write something down on a piece of paper, using the lockers for support. Figuring I've misinterpreted his actions, I turn my attention back to Brett.

"That being said, how's my favorite little freshman buddy today?" he inquires, full of charm as always.

My face flushes a deep red as our eyes meet, causing me to struggle for a reply, "Alright, I guess."

"Only alright, huh?" he acknowledges, a dramatic expression of worry flashing across his chestnut eyes. "What's the matter?"

Scratching the back of my neck, I stall, attempting to sort out a response without tripping over my own words. "Well, I'm kinda nervous about this thing I have to do for Mrs. Griffin's class for fourth period. She's making us recite an original poem in class today, and I'm not sure if mine's good enough."

"Really? But don't you love to write? I see you sitting at that picnic table in your backyard with different composition books all the time. I bet it's more amazing than you think!"

My mind freezes solid for a second, stunned at his acknowledgment. Realizing that he has, in fact, noticed me after all these years of not knowing if he was even aware of my first name makes my cheeks produce a darker pink tint. "You think so?"

"Yeah, you seem like the imaginative type. I bet that's why you're always so quiet, right? You're always coming up with something new to write about."

"Yeah, I guess that's part of the reason." I laugh, still halfway stuck in my love-struck daze. "But usually people don't like the creative types. I know a lot of people think we're spazzy or insane. That's why I usually don't tell people I like to write. I mean you should've seen the looks they were giving me in science yesterday after Mr. Donoghue made us introduce ourselves."

Brett shakes his head. "Well, some people may be stupid like that, but I'm not. Actually, a girl with an imagination is pretty cool if you ask me. They're mysterious and hard to figure out, and honestly, I've always liked that about you." My face lights up like a young child's on Christmas morning at his remark, though my dream world crashes to an end as we reach our classes.

"So I guess I'll see you again tomorrow morning?" he asks, bearing the smile that has melted a hundred girls' hearts.

"You know it!" I agree too quickly, failing to mask my enthusiasm. A glint of amusement flashes across Brett's eyes as he enters his class, hopefully not due to my eagerness.

Whew, I'm finally able to breathe properly again. This morning has already exceeded perfection. Even in my daydreams about Brett, I've never imagined him saying anything that flattering, especially about my writing. This miraculous, magnificent conversation will be going down in my diary word for word. There's no doubt in my mind that if things keep progressing like this, Brett will soon be mine.

⌘

By the time lunch rolls around, I conclude that I have been blessed with a pretty awesome day, with the exception of my growing anxiety about fourth period. I sigh, cringing at the thought of presenting, and head toward the lunch line.

Standing on my own for a few minutes behind two upperclassmen, I'm constructing a couple rhymes in my head for my next poem, when I overhear a familiar voice say my name from further ahead in line. Skimming through the faces, I locate Trent near the midpoint, where he's talking to Carter. I won't lie, this peaks my interest. Unfortunately, since a group of sophomore girls is squealing at full volume behind me about some flirty text message, all chances of eavesdropping on Trent are shot. Finally, the noisemakers grow silent at the exact moment Trent launches into an exasperated rant, "Carter, for the last time, she's not dating anyone! I know you kinda have this thing for her—even though you barely know her, which is still rather weird in my opinion. But then again, you've never liked anyone like that. So go for it, dude!"

A shower of awkwardness descends upon me like the rains that caused Noah's flood. Yesterday when I met Carter,

I hadn't considered him in a romantic way. I mean he's nice enough, but Brett's in the picture now. I've liked him on the verge of seven years now; there's no way I'm about to let the consideration of a guy I've known for a day get in the way of that.

Minutes later, I receive my food and proceed back to the table I sat at yesterday, not feeling like searching for another seat. Still, no one bothers to look up when I sit down, no one says anything, and I continue on with my lunch, frazzled about what I've overheard.

⌘

The fourth period bell summons me to face my fears soon after. I end up choosing the same desk I did yesterday, with Taylor opting to sit next to me.

"So, what's your poem about?" she asks, pulling the paper copy we're to submit to Mrs. Griffin out of her binder.

"Well, if I'm being honest, it's about this guy I like," I confess lowly.

"Does he go to school here?" Taylor's gray eyes widen, intrigued.

"Yeah, but I'd rather not say who he is; I'm not sure if he feels the same way about me yet. Actually, he talked to me for the first time yesterday, so it's way too early to tell."

"Oh, gotcha! Well, good luck; maybe he'll ask you out soon!"

Standing up from her desk at the front of the room, Mrs. Griffin claps her hands together, signaling for us to listen up. She asks if anyone would like to volunteer to recite their poem first, and someone in the back named Sage takes the bait. Her poem, entitled "Lemuropolosis" ends up being about the world coming to an end in graphic detail. Zombies ate brains, humans were subjecting themselves to cannibalism, and the President of the United States was kidnapped by an invasion of lemurs sent in from Madagascar. I can tell by her face that Mrs. Griffin thinks it is borderline insane, but she admits that it was well written.

"She delivers a dystopian masterpiece, and I could barely manage to write a stanza about my dog. It's safe to say I need to stick to short stories," Taylor mumbles to me, though not low enough to escape the trained ears of Mrs. Griffin.

"Miss Newcomb, would you like to share that poem with us?" Mrs. Griffin suggests, making Taylor wince. Full of reluctance, she grabs her copy of "A Dog Named Sparrow" and proceeds to recite. The poem's not as bad as she lets on, and we find out her dog is named Sparrow after her favorite character from *Pirates of the Caribbean*, which is pretty epic.

Can't Beat the Heart of a Carolina Girl

The majority of the class recite their poems before Mrs. Griffin calls on me. My legs quake beneath me as I make my way to the front of the class, though when I reach the podium my nerves recede at the memory of Brett's comment this morning. Regaining confidence in myself, I begin:

"Behind your blue eyes, I can see what we could be.

Behind your blue eyes, I can tell you want to be with me.

But what will others think?

They see no connection between you and me.

They just don't know us.

Behind your blue eyes, I can tell you're afraid.

You want us to be together, but what will others say?

And behind my blue eyes, I feel your pain.

There's nothing we can do and all I can say,

Is that I love you.

Behind my blue eyes, I don't want to hide my love for you,

But what others might think is what's causing me to.

Behind my blue eyes, I hope you see the truth;

The true love, that lies within me."

"Excellent work, Miss Houston. I've always been a sucker for a good love poem." Mrs. Griffin smiles, writing down comments on the paper copy I handed her for grading purposes.

Upon returning to my desk, Carter waves at me from the seat behind mine. I hadn't even noticed him come in this afternoon or yesterday, if I'm being completely truthful. He offers a warm smile when I acknowledge him, and I return one to be friendly, though it occurs to me that I may have a new stalker to worry about. Mrs. Griffin goes down our row asking him to present his poem next, filling me with relief.

Carter clears his throat, glancing up in my direction for a millisecond before reciting his piece:

"I see you walking with a friend;

Maybe you're nothing more.

Even though it may be just that,

My heart is still sore.

I've known you not long at all,

Yet my feelings for you are anything but small.

Forever longing for the day when you'll be mine,

Maybe you'll hear me out with this sign.

I've never before considered romance,

Can't Beat the Heart of a Carolina Girl

All I ask from you is a chance."

The way his eyes flutter up at me again upon uttering the last line connect the last few dots for me. This is what Carter was writing at his locker this morning in the hallway after Brett asked me to walk with him! My cheeks burn as he makes his way back to his seat. Staring down at my desk, I don't know how to take Carter's obvious feelings for me.

The remaining students in class either recite their work or are lectured for not having a poem prepared before the last bell chimes. Throughout the rest of the class, I could feel Carter staring at the back of my head, making me uncomfortable. My heart aches for leading him on, although I have no idea exactly *how* I've led him on. Ugh, this is all Trent's fault!

As Mrs. Griffin is attempting to be heard over the roar of students packing up, informing us to read the first two chapters of the novel *Of Mice and Men* for homework, I throw my binder into my bookbag, rushing out the door as quickly as possible. I've heard enough of the affections of my not-so-secret admirer today, and the pick-up area is beckoning me like a safe haven. Waiting in front of the school building, I can hear the soft tread of sneakers coming up from behind me. Glancing over my shoulder I find none other than who? Of course, Carter.

"Hey, Riley." He nods, rubbing the back of his neck. Meeting his gaze, his blue eyes shine at me like warning beacons. Crap.

"Hey, Carter," I return, breaking eye contact. No need to build his hopes up that I reciprocate his feelings.

"Well, I was just gonna tell you that... um... I liked your poem. You're an awesome router—dang it, I mean writer." He grimaces, embarrassed that he fumbled the compliment.

Despite myself, I can't help but smile at his struggle for words. Turning to face him again, he regains eye contact. "You have really pretty eyes," he blurts. I must be unable to conceal my surprise, for his cheeks highlight under pressure. "Sorry," he mumbles, kicking at a pebble with the toe of his shoe.

Giggling a little, I emphasize, "It's no problem." Has anyone ever been this nervous around me? It's obvious this kid wants to talk to me, so I drop my harsh front. "Hey, guess what?"

"What?" he manages, not daring to look at me.

"You have really pretty eyes, too."

For whatever reason, I'm enjoying this more than I should. At last, Carter faces me again, grinning with relief. Honestly, he's not that bad. Sure, he doesn't dress like the majority of the traditionally attractive guys at Linwood Whaley High—a mix of preppy, athletic, or redneck, sometimes all on the same person—though his flannel over T-shirt combination is starting to grow on me. I hate to admit it, but now that I'm getting a better look at him, he may actually be cuter than Brett. His boyish smile is inviting, making him seem approachable, whereas Brett's traveling gaze sometimes leaves me feeling as if I'm bothering him. Regardless, I can't let this guy waltz in and ruin my chances of being with Brett, no matter how cute or nice he may be.

Chapter Five

"And so then, Sawyer and I were stuck on this back road out of gas and out of money, with like half a bag of Doritos and about an hour to waste since Will sucks at navigating. He was our only hope of getting back by curfew without our parents knowing," Brett snorts, rehashing his tale from Saturday night as we approach our classroom doors this morning. We've been walking to class together for a couple months now, and I'm still pretty dang psyched about it every time I see him waiting for me near Mrs. Wilson's door after homeroom.

"I thought I heard you speed into your driveway that night!" I exclaim, not realizing how stalkerish the words seem until they leave my mouth. Looking away, I silently chastise myself.

"Oh, did you?" Brett grins, leaning against the brick wall outside his Accounting class, raising an eyebrow. "You do that often?"

"What do you mean?" I try to remain nonchalant, busying myself by pulling at the hem of my shirt.

"Wait up for me to come home like that?"

Laughing at his confident remark, I allow myself to bluff through my lie. "Please, don't flatter yourself! Your truck's exhaust woke me up. You know how loud that thing is."

"Uh huh, if you say so." He laughs, winking at me. The bell rings, notifying us to wrap up our conversation. Turning to enter my class, Brett stops me in my tracks. "You know, if you did, though, that'd be pretty cute if you ask me."

Smiling to myself, I don't even bother to turn around to refute any further, merely proceeding into the classroom and leaving him alone to wonder for himself.

⌘

In Earth Science this afternoon, Mr. Donoghue puts on a video entitled *The Great Wonders of Natural Disasters* and leaves the classroom for forty-five minutes to grab some snacks from the teacher's lounge. Being that Taylor's out sick with strep throat and Trent's conked out in a cold sleep on his desk drooling away the class period, I decide to break out my notebook and write some poetry that may or may not be inspired by the events of this morning.

As I'm jotting down line after line as they come to me, it feels as if someone is boring a hole through the side of my head. Glancing around, I catch Carter's swift motion, turning back to the novel he's not exactly enthralled with. I continue to watch him from my vantage point, being that he has to turn around to be able to see me from his seat. Less than a minute passes before he stretches back in his chair, leaning in a way that allows him to have a perfect view of my seat. Waving at him, I aim to let him know I'm amused at his inconspicuous nature. His eyes widen in fear when he realizes I've caught him staring, causing him to jerk back to face the front with enough force that the novel soars right off his desk, sending it sliding across the floor toward me. Seizing the opportunity, I pick up the book for him, dusting the dirt from it before returning it to Carter.

"I believe you dropped this, sir." I can't help but giggle at his expense.

Carter replies with a slight nod, not daring to risk adding an unintentionally embarrassing comment at this point. I hate to leave him in agony like this; thanks to a certain Mr. Harvey, I'm well-accustomed to mortifying moments like this. Instead, I make an effort to ease his mind. "I don't think you're a creeper Carter, if that's what you're thinking. Don't worry about it; I've been there, too," I whisper, smiling as I pat his hand. His downcast eyes light up as I do so, giving him the confidence to say something.

"Sorry about that." He laughs softly, shaking off nerves. "I saw you writing and it caught my attention. Trent told me that you're a pretty good writer, and like I said before, that poem you wrote for English was awesome in my opinion.

Would you mind if I read some of your other poems sometime?"

I swallow, somewhat awestruck by his question. Only a handful of people ever remembers the fact that I love poetry, and an even smaller percentage has ever taken the time to read my pieces. Well, if you even consider Momma's sole reading of one poem to be a percentage. Of course, I wouldn't mind if he read them; the fact that he likes to read himself could allow for some insight as what I need to fix. Thinking back to the two short poems I've written in class, however, I recall that Brett is the subject for both. Lord knows Carter doesn't need to read those right now.

"I wouldn't mind at all. You're actually the first person outside of my family to ever ask me that," I return, swiping my hair behind my ear, growing nervous at the mention, "but I'll have to show you some older ones sometime. The ones I wrote today aren't that great. They could use some editing."

"An artist and her work." Carter smiles, leaning back in his chair. "Yeah, that sounds great, just let me know! I'm sure the ones you wrote today are better than you think, though."

"Thanks," I reply, patting his desk again. "Well, I'll see you around."

En route back to my desk, I take a quick glimpse back over at Carter once I reach my row, where he's waving at me in the same manner I did a few minutes ago. *Goodness gracious,* I muse as I return his wave, *this boy is something else.*

⌘

"You look so beautiful tonight, Riley."

I clear my throat, still amazed that I've been living this miracle for the last three hours. I mean, what other word can I use to describe it? Here I am, sitting in the backyard with none other than Brett Harvey himself, snuggled up with him under a blanket of stars. After eating a picnic lunch together, we've enjoyed an evening of admiring God's handiwork in the sky, taking in the clouds, the sunset, and now the wonders of the galaxy.

"You've said that three times already." I'm rendered breathless, watching as the starlight illuminates his eyes.

"It doesn't stop it from being true," his voice grows soft, leaning in to get a better view of my face. He brings his hand to my chin, tilting my head to face him. After seven years of waiting, this moment has arrived at last.

Yet, as our lips meet, uncertainty washes over me. It's not that he's a bad kisser or anything, but my intuition throws up red flags. Despite my best efforts to relish in the fact that the guy I've pined after all this time ultimately returns my feelings, nothing about this feels right. Overwhelmed by my thoughts, my eyes pop open in the midst of our kiss.

"Isn't this everything you've ever wanted?" I hear Brett's voice fading in the distance. The darkness has encompassed us both, denying me the ability to see him. Throwing my arms out, I search aimlessly throughout the surrounding area, desperate to locate him. A hand grabs mine seconds later, warm to the touch.

"Looks like you've found me," a voice replies, blue eyes shining in the night as the person draws nearer. Before me now stands Carter, with Brett nowhere in sight.

"Carter, what are you doing here? Where'd Brett go?" I ask in vain, peering around to find that we're the only two in the vicinity.

"Turns out he's far from what you've imagined, Riles," Carter explains, pulling me closer, "but a certain source has told me that I'm not." Caressing my cheek, he leans into me, his lips gentle as they press against my own. Shooting stars decorate the sky as if they are fireworks, sparks making my heart jump like bang... bang... bang...

BEEP *BEEP* *BEEP*

Jolting upright in bed, my hand slaps down on my alarm clock in a panic, nearly knocking it off my bedside table. What the heck was that all about?

⌘

In all my years of feeling awkward in front of a crowd of people, I've never felt this out of place entering a classroom before. Turning the knob to enter Earth Science this afternoon after that bombshell and a half of a dream, I secretly hope that Carter's not at school today. Well, that, coupled with the lingering memory of that kiss, albeit imaginary, has me wishing that he'll be up to his usual antics of admiring me from afar.

Another surprise emerges from out of the blue when Mr. Donoghue pulls up a PowerPoint presentation for chapter seven and begins going over the material with us. Not that he hasn't done this before, though it's been a rare occurrence in the last few weeks, what with Cook Out opening within a mile from the school. Either I'm accustomed to not learning in this class, or that dream has had a more haunting effect on me than I thought, as I keep finding my line of vision flitting over in Carter's direction every few minutes. Thankfully, he's paying attention to Mr. Donoghue, taking notes on the material as I should be doing.

Further distracting me from the lecture, my heart jumps as my phone vibrates in my jacket pocket. Knowing that

Can't Beat the Heart of a Carolina Girl

Mr. Donoghue could care less if we're on our phones or not, I slide the phone out of my pocket, flipping it open in anticipation. Why is my heart sinking as I read the name *Brett Harvey* on the screen?

Brett: Hey Riley, missed u this morning. Where were u?

I cringe, hoping he's not too bothered by the fact that I scurried off to class this morning without so much as peeking around the hall to find him. But hey, after that dream can you blame me?

Riley: Sorry about that. Had to get to Career Management early to study last minute for a test.

Brett: Oh no big deal I understand. I just wanted to ask u something?

Riley: Yeah sure?

Brett: Wanna go see a movie this weekend?

Sheer shock overtakes me as my phone falls onto my desk with a solid thud. Though Mr. Donoghue couldn't hear it over the sound of his own rambling, it catches Carter's attention. Shooting me a puzzled glance when he notices I'm already looking his way causes me to divert my attention back to my phone. Hesitantly, I type my reply.

Riley: Yeah that sounds fun!

I mean, how accurate can a dream be, anyway?

Chapter Six

"Alright, so I've been dying to see this one for months. Brady Dunham is in it, and I swear it looks better than that one he did last summer with Will Ferrell! He's my favorite actor," Brett continues to ramble as we're on our way to Grahamwood's miniscule excuse of a movie theater across town. Under normal circumstances, I'd be thrilled that we've got a chance to talk on the way to and from the movies, but after the dream I had featuring Brett and Carter, my first "date" with Brett is not turning out like I've always pictured. For instance, I never would've thought I'd be distracted by thinking about another guy while I'm sitting in the passenger's seat of Brett's Chevy, but here I am.

"That's cool," I utter, attempting to contribute to the conversation despite my lack of interest in it. Don't get me wrong, a lot of people consider Brady Dunham to be the greatest comedic genius in Hollywood since Robin Williams, but I'm not a big fan of Dunham's films because he always acts juvenile and the content is somewhat vulgar in my opinion. I try to avoid watching stuff like that at all costs. How did I not know that Brett was such a fan of him?

"Yeah… um hey, are you alright? You're being mighty quiet," Brett inquires, casting me a sideways glance as he flicks his turn signal to get into the passing lane.

"Yeah, I am. Sorry, I'm just, I don't know. I've got a lot on my mind right now," I cover, tucking a strand of hair behind my ear.

"Good things I hope?" he requests, his eyes full of optimism. Unsure how to respond, I flash him a half-smile and a shrug. "Well, that's not much of a positive answer," he says, reaching over to grab my hand. My eyes widen at the gesture as he interlocks his fingers with mine. "But maybe the movie will make you laugh and help you relax."

Fat chance, I'm quick to judge, though I scold myself afterward. I haven't seen this movie, so who am I to judge whether it's funny or not? What the heck is wrong with me? Why am I even finding fault with this date? The guy I've been crushing on for seven years is holding my hand right now, and all I can think about is that stupid dream that holds no true meaning whatsoever. It's a figment of my imagination. Was I even feeling disconnected from Brett before that dream? Nope. And at this realization, I make an effort to encourage my original wishes.

"I think it will." I squeeze his hand. "So, tell me more about this movie."

⌘

Can't Beat the Heart of a Carolina Girl

Brett's still cackling every few minutes about the, by his definition, hilarious scenes which consisted of some of the most obscene language I've ever heard in my fourteen years of life as we're on our way home tonight. The movie was only rated PG-13, but I know that my parents would blush at the film we saw. Ugh, I cringe just thinking about it; it was easily the grossest movie I've ever seen.

"So, enough about that," Brett comments as we pass the elementary school, the midpoint between downtown and home. He studies me in the radio lights, donning a heart-melting half-smile. "Have I told you that you look beautiful tonight, Riley?"

As if the fact that he held my hand again at the movies and has reached for it a third time once he maneuvered the truck out of the parking lot didn't startle me enough, the expression of surprise I shoot back at him says it all. Where have I heard that before? I stare at him like a dumbfounded idiot for a matter of seconds before remembering to reply, "No, but thank you."

"You're welcome. I mean, it's true after all," he admits, winking at me.

Come on now, I should be enjoying this! Why, instead, is a sharp panic seeping through my veins? Contrary to what I'm thinking, I take a deep breath, attempting to rid myself of these doubts once and for all tonight. It's time to cut to the chase. "So, what made you want to ask me to hang out tonight?"

As soon as my words register, Brett clears his throat. Did something I say actually make him nervous? Ha, this is getting good! "Well, um… we have been talking a lot at school lately," he explains, running his available hand through his hair as he comes to a halt at a stoplight, "and well, I'm just going to throw it out there. You've charmed me, Riley."

The grin he's flashing my way, the stars that are twinkling above us at this red light, the way he's running his thumb over my knuckles… this is how I've fantasized this moment happening for the better half of a decade. My previous notions of doubt vanish from my mind as I smile back at him, relishing the moment before I allow myself to speak. Finally, after I fear that the beating of my heart will soon grow loud enough for him to hear, I realize that I don't know how to respond to that! Do I tell him I like him back? Do I say thank you? None of my daydreams ever prepared me for this! The light flashes green again, and a somewhat wary Brett is now pressing the gas, sending us forward and diverting his attention back to the road. An extensive awkward silence proceeds throughout the cab before I finally blurt, "Ditto."

Brett's reaction speaks volumes as he turns to face me again, his eyes wide in bewilderment. "Ditto?"

Resorting back to my native ways, my cheeks pull a chameleon act, producing the same color as the previous red light. Doing my best to recover from my act of stupidity, I reply, "I mean I've liked you for a while, too."

"Yeah?" He seems intrigued, which I take as a good sign. "Since when?"

Alright, it's either time to lie straight to his face or allow him to meet his number one stalker. Dropping my gaze, I admit the words I've been hiding from him since our friendship began on the first day of school. "Since I was eight."

The words leave my lips as if I'm striking a match to ignite dynamite, as if I plan on erupting the entire situation by dropping this truth. Silence explodes throughout the truck, further heightening my fears. I turn to look out the passenger's side window, averting his sight for all intents and purposes.

After what seems like a quarter of eternity, Brett returns, "Awesome." I have no indication as to whether he took that in a positive or negative way, but nonetheless, the smile of relief that floods over my face suggests that tonight is going down in history regardless.

⌘

Not so much to my surprise, my elated demeanor has remained through the weekend, as noted in my diary and bragging to my sister, who in turn gagged loudly and proceeded to exit the room. I couldn't care less though, for my daydreams have finally become a reality. Though the remainder of the ride home was a little on the quiet side after our admittance of mutual affection, Brett's been texting me nonstop ever since, mirroring the behavior of the smile that has graced my face since Friday night. As I walk into Mr. Donoghue's class today, apparently everyone else can tell something's up; as soon as I sit down, Taylor prods for information.

"I know that smile anywhere. That is the smile of a love-stricken goober!" Her grin is mischievous as she nudges my arm.

"What, this?" I feign, sticking my tongue out at her.

"Not funny, Houston. I need details, stat."

"Oh, alright," I begin, hoping a tired sign can deter her interest, but those gray eyes are trained on me like an eagle. "So I've been talking to Brett Harvey and…"

Taylor's eyes light up, finally cracking the case of whom I've been crushing on for the last few months. "I knew it! He's the one that the poem for English was about!" she whispers, hoping her predictions are correct. Since we've become fast friends within the last couple months, I can't keep this secret from her any longer, so I affirm the notion with a nod.

"Yes! Okay, so now why are you grinning like a raccoon on refrigerator clean-out day?"

"Well, um… I guess you could say we went on this date Frid—"

49

Can't Beat the Heart of a Carolina Girl

"Seriously? No way!" Taylor slaps her desk, causing Carter to look over at us from his seat. "Sorry," she adds immediately, shifting her eyes around in case she caught the attention of some others. "Please don't mind if I live vicariously through your new romantic escapades. Things with my own crush are going absolutely nowhere. It's Will Shepard, the junior? The guy who makes Ryan Gosling seem unattractive? The one who I always manage to choke on air around whenever I get within five feet of him in the halls?" Taylor discloses shamefaced, burying her humiliation in the sleeve of her olive cardigan. I force a subtle laugh before she lifts her hand up, urging me to continue my tale.

"Well..." I glance around, inadvertently meeting Carter's gaze before resuming. I feel like I'm relaying government secrets or something, as I know he doesn't need to hear this. "He texted me while I was in class the other day and asked me to go see a movie with him on Friday night. So I went, and he ended up holding my hand most of the night, and," I continue, dreading this final blow for Carter's sake, "in a way, he told me that he likes me."

Taylor signs a thumbs up from her face-plant position on the desk, mumbling, "Go, girl, go!" which causes me to laugh again. Nevertheless, the air of despondency on the brown-haired boy in my peripheral vision causes it to subside. Of all the times I've imagined retelling the fairy tale I witnessed on Friday night, never once did it occur to me that my happiness with the guy of my dreams would only inflict daggers of heartbreak on someone else.

⌘

"Ya done broke the boy's heart, Riles."

Trent, as usual, oh-so-delicately decides to break the news I was already aware of the Wednesday night following my proclamation in Earth Science as soon as he takes a seat beside me in Youth Group. The looks the remaining students are giving me are priceless, more or less because I'm sure they never thought I could get a date, let alone break a heart. But that in itself is an entirely different matter.

"Come on, it wasn't like it was intentional!" I breathe, resting my head in my palm as I refocus my attention to our Bible study book.

"Please. If you would have been the decent cousin I assumed you were, you would have told me that you had a crush on Brett the Terrible way back when, so I wouldn't have been advertising your case to Carter for, oh, I don't know… since the sixth grade!"

"Shh… dude, do you mind?" I whisper in a harsh tone, flicking his arm for announcing to the entirety of Youth Group who the object of my affection is. And, being that Grahamwood is as small as a gnat in the grand scheme of things and that everyone now coincidentally has their cell phones out with their fingers poised on the keypads, I assume this is going to spread like wildfire.

"No, actually I don't!" my cousin hisses, though lowering his voice regardless. He eyes the other kids as if daring them to text their friends about what he said before he continues, "Because when we were all in the sixth grade, you had convinced me otherwise, and someone was rather smitten with you."

"What the heck are you talking about? I didn't even know Carter back then!"

"Yes, you did!" Trent huffs, rifling through the pockets on his over-sized sports jacket to reveal a photograph. "My eleventh birthday party, at the skating rink. The short boy with the glasses?" He jabs his index finger at a kid standing to the left of his younger self. "The one that helped you up when you nearly busted your butt in the middle of the rink like the *Lizzie McGuire* clone you are?"

"Yes, I remember the party. Your point, Trent?!" I steam, growing more irritated by the second.

"It was Carter!" he hashes, throwing up his hands for emphasis. "Y'all didn't meet in Earth Science; you met three years ago. And back then Carter—being an even bigger nerd than he is now—developed quite a crush on you that day, young lady."

"Wha—"

52

"Let me finish! He's my best friend, and you're my best cousin, or so I thought. So when he started asking about you after that day, I was psyched. Because wouldn't that be amazing, getting two of your all-time favorite people together? And you ruined it with Brett Harvey of all people, you dream crusher."

Rolling my eyes, I glare back up. "Well, if you wanted Carter and me to get together so bad, why the heck didn't you ever tell me about him?" I retort, tired of being the villain in a situation I hadn't wanted any part in. "Plus, when have you ever asked me if I had a crush on someone? I mean dang, I'm sorry I don't remember the dude from one time three years ago, but—"

"Because he's never had any intention of actually trying to talk to you... well, until this year," Trent admits, running his hand over his face. "Back then, he was pretty insecure. He got made fun of a lot because he was too small to play football or basketball; the guys at our school were absolute jerks to him. But over the summer, he got taller, switched to contacts, and pretty much the week before school started asked me to help him out with getting to know you. Thus began our story of The Awkward and The Loveless."

I stare at him, incredulous of what I'm hearing. "So the whole thing in Mr. Donoghue's class the first day, that wasn't your scheme? It was all his idea?"

"Yes, did you not catch that from my rant?"

Resisting the urge to slap him, I want to continue, though I'm at a loss for words. This entire semester, this crush hasn't been some spur of the moment thing for Carter. He's been nervous about this, meditated on it even before daring to take that risk. That's rather noble of him, I suppose. But still, that's not any reason to incite guilt on me for pursuing Brett, either. Instead, I remain silent, pondering this new flood of information until our Youth Group leader walks in, praying that all of this has no correlation with that crazy dream.

Chapter Seven

Seeing November on all the calendars makes me find it hard to believe that my movie date with Brett was three weeks ago. This little—I don't know what to call our new dynamic, actually—is still going strong. He's even started texting me things like "good morning beautiful!" which absolutely make my day. I don't know when he's planning on asking me to be his girlfriend, but I pray it's soon. The suspense is driving me bonkers!

As for my other aficionado, the poor sap has been relentless, staring at me the same way Gollum beholds his Precious in *Lord of the Rings*. He's so obvious, it isn't even funny. Trent even told him to lay off the other day (quite loudly, I might add), even after the lecture he gave me in Youth Group. Oh well, he's incited a borderline stalkerish monster!

Right now, I'm dreading every ounce of boredom in my second period computer class, anxious for Thanksgiving break to get here in a couple days. I glance up at the wall clock for the fifth time wondering when the teacher will be returning from the main office, when a guy named Joel rolls his chair over to mine.

"Hey, Riley! Guess what I overheard?"

Can't Beat the Heart of a Carolina Girl

"What Joel?" I ask, trying not to stare at the tape on his glasses. If you were to ask Hailey, he's the biggest nerd in school; if you were to ask Jeremy, he's the easiest target in school. Nevertheless, the guy I've come to know over the past few months—who reminds me of the teenage Chuckie Finster from *All Grown Up!*, minus the wild locks of red hair— is one of the nicest kids from Grahamwood, and has served as an excellent tutor in all things techy.

"Well, you know, since I help out with IT after school, I'm able to catch some pretty juicy news from the main office," he drags along.

"Joel, please hurry and tell me before Ms. Mitchell comes back!" I plead. Don't get me wrong, she's a super nice teacher, but she is relentless when she finds someone talking instead of working on assignments.

"Well, yesterday, I heard we're getting a new girl in our class today!"

"Really? When is she coming? Class is like half over."

Right about the time those words leave my lips, Ms. Mitchell sticks her head through the half-open door. Peering in our direction, she flips her lid seeing that Joel has rolled halfway across the classroom.

"Joel Connors, unless you're instructing Miss Houston on how to run a search query in a database, I suggest you return to your seat," Ms. Mitchell demands, casting him a look so stone cold she could be mistaken for Medusa.

"Yes, ma'am!" Joel screeches, pushing off my desk to send his rolling chair sailing across the tiled floor.

Ms. Mitchell sighs in anxiety, smoothing out a wrinkle in her knee-length skirt. "Now class, since we've all settled down, I'd like to introduce our new student... Miss Thomas." A girl reaching about 5'1" walks into the classroom. Dark hair adorns her head, reminding me of my best friend that moved away back in fourth grade, though there's no way it could be her. Lexie's last name is Albertson.

"Now, Miss Thomas, you can sit over there next to um... let me think... it's Kiley, right?" Ms. Mitchell continues, pointing to the available computer next to mine.

"It's Riley, Ms. Mitchell," I correct, though she fails to hear me. I've been in this class for three months and my own teacher can't remember my name? Well, that's what you get when you're Riley Houston.

The girl makes her way over to the designated seat, speaking to me as she does so. "Hey, you must be Riley?" She takes a binder decorated with pictures of Dachshunds out of her bookbag, placing it on the desk before her.

"Yeah, and thanks for getting my name right by the way," I reply, attempting to make light of our teacher's mishap.

"Oh, it's no problem. I had a friend with that name a long time ago, but then I moved to Indiana. I haven't been able to keep in touch with her though, unfortunately. But, when we were younger, we made these friendship bracelets for each other." She holds her arm out for me to see.

Inhaling a sharp breath, I take in the purple and orange beaded bracelet that matches the one on my left arm. "It's just like mine!" Pulling up my hoodie sleeve, I show her.

"Oh gosh, Riley!" Lexie shrieks, "You look so different, I didn't even recognize you!" Ms. Mitchell shoots us a disgruntled look, so we decide to catch up later.

So, after years of being a lonely, hideous, friendless loser, things are starting to work out for me. But still, I can't shake the feeling that something is about to throw my long-awaited perfect world into a portal of chaos.

⌘

Soon Introduction to Computers ends for the day, and my reunited best friend and I go our separate ways to our third period classes: World History for Lexie and Earth Science for me with you know who. Of course, Carter.

You know, despite my not-so-secret admirer, Earth Science is my favorite class. It's super easy, and Mr. Donoghue never assigns much work, so every other day ends up being a free period. That usually means Jesse tries to convince Jeremy that UNC's basketball team is better than Duke's, Tiffany and Nichole text each other when they're sitting right next to one another, and Queen Carson sits in the back of the room talking on her cell phone to Jennifer, the senior cheerleader, about which football player she'll date next. Oh, and to fill the awkward quota, I get stared at for ninety minutes by Mr. Carter Pickett.

Today we have a substitute teacher, who—like Mr. Donoghue—ends up taking a nap in the desk chair. Taylor and I put our desks together and make up funny picture stories to pass the time, as we've taken to doing a lot lately. Honestly, I don't know how Mrs. Carothers can sleep through it all, what with everyone talking at once. While she naps her way to her next paycheck, Hailey can be heard over everyone as she's retelling the conversation she had with Jennifer to Tiffany.

"So I was like ohmigosh you, like, can't be serious! Brett Harvey was soooo checking me out at the game last night, but Jen was like, 'No girl, he totally, like, does *not* like you!' But I, like, know *for real* that he's, like, *totally* in love with me!" Hailey brags, twirling her dark brown hair around a manicured finger. If looks could kill, my glare could disintegrate that cell phone in her hand. She's been running her trap about Brett all week! No one thinks she stands a chance, being that Brett's a little too tough and rugged to be interested in someone as superficial as her. But then again, he is the quarterback on the football team, and cheerleaders have always been their kryptonite. I make a mental note to keep an eye out for that, especially since Brett and I are on the verge of becoming a couple.

"One day she's gonna use up the entire oxygen supply with her whiny narratives, causing us to die at her expense," I hash, burying my head in the folds of my arms.

Taylor covers her mouth with her hand to keep from chuckling. "I take it that reality show reject annoys you as much as she does me?"

"Let's just say you'd win big on that bet."

"I don't know why she keeps talking about Brett, anyway," Taylor continues, adding small details to one of the drawings on our picture story about a cat named Pedro who drives a monster truck. "He's way out of her league. Especially in the decency department. Plus, he's obviously taken by your adorableness!"

I smile, thinking about all the sweet things Brett's told me throughout the last few weeks. "Amen! Thanks, Taylor," I sigh.

"Ry, Ry! Over here!"

Despite my longing to forbid them from gaining my attention, I turn see Tiffany beckoning me over to where she and Hailey are sitting. Looking back at Taylor first in an attempt to ignore them, I hope she'll give up. Yet, she persists in calling my name in that nails-on-a-chalkboard-like voice of hers. For the sake of my nerves, I stand in reluctance, making my way back there so she'll shut up.

"Hello, Riley." Hailey scoffs upon my arrival at her throne.

"You summoned?" I counter, matching her hateful tone. Normally I wouldn't put my hatred for her on public display, but the Brett talk is really starting to irritate me.

"I heard that you and Brett Harvey have been quite chummy lately, is that right?"

Is she serious right now? "Yeah kinda, what about it?"

"Well, I know how desperate you are for a guy that you would probably go out with Jody from homeroom, but anyone can tell Brett isn't interested in a Miss Loner. He wants me, so put those generic Converse to good use and walk away from him now."

I swear a vein pops in my neck. What have I ever done to her to warrant such hostility? Without thinking, I drop my filter and let her have it.

"First of all, why is it any of your concern that Brett and I are talking? Besides, he told me himself that I've charmed him!" Sure, it's none of her business, but I love the presence of intense rage forming on her brow.

"Second, I am not desperate for a guy. Sure, I've never dated anyone, but I'm perfectly fine with that. Besides, I'm not interested in dating Joel, but I do consider him to be a good friend. And for your information, that's his name. Joel, not Jody, and he's not a dork, or a nerd, or whatever name you've anointed him with lately. Oh, and I'd rather know I paid a solid fifteen dollars for these shoes than live my life in debt like you'll do after your parents cut you off, you reality show reject." I scorch her ego, thankful that Taylor's previous comment was still fresh in my mind. "You can tell me to do whatever you may jolly well please Shug, but I'm done being afraid of you. You're an empty threat."

A sense of empowerment showers over me, though it soon dissipates as I realize that the whole class has grown silent to listen to my rant. Turning a deep shade of scarlet, I scurry back to my desk like a squirrel avoiding getting squashed by an eighteen-wheeler. Both Hailey and Tiffany remain baffled with their big mouths agape, speechless for once.

Plopping back down in my seat, Taylor shoots me a thumbs up. The class remains silent until Jeremy can't hold back his laughter anymore. "Dang Houston, look what you've been hiding all these years! Tell her how it is!" Hailey snaps, appearing as if she's going to backhand him if it wouldn't break her nail. The rest of the class joins in, congratulating me for finally putting her in her place. I laugh along, stating that it was no big deal, though I'd be lying if I said I'm not proud of myself too.

Stepping up to the front of the class a few minutes later, Hailey finally deliberates a "master plan" rebuttal to settle her case. "Well Riley, since you're so confident in the fact that Brett only has eyes for you, and you're happy being single anyway, how would you feel if I... oh, I don't know... ask him out? You know, just for fun?" An evil grin surfaces on her overly contoured face, and I promise I could knock her upside the head with something hard, but there are too many witnesses.

Obviously, I'm faced with a dilemma here. If I tell her no, she'll continue to humiliate me for the rest of my life, because I can't go back on my words after a kick-butt rant like that. If I tell her yes, there's a chance that she might get her wish, despite all that I know about Brett. In that case, I'll be heartbroken, more so in that I literally enabled her to go about doing it. The tension building in my throat as I conjure up a response is making me nauseous, but then I remember how Brett mentioned he likes girls with a mysterious flair about them! If I know anything about him, he won't be fazed by her assertion because she's as transparent as they come. Weighing my options, I decide this is the best possibility.

"Well, Riley? I want an answer today!" Hailey nags, examining her nails.

"You know what? Go ahead!" I permit, waving my hands in exasperation. "Go ask Brett out! You don't need my permission, unless you actually are as worried about other people's opinions of you, as we all believe you are," I refute, mirroring the evil grin she has plastered on her face.

Everyone interjects with that stupid "ooh" noise that sounds like a gorilla calling through a cave, while Trent snorts, "Good burn, Riles!"

"Thanks, Trent," I reply, leaning back in my chair. Yet again, Hailey stands speechless, taking a moment before storming off to her group. Realizing my chance for a moment of peace, I release a nervous breath I've been holding in. Maybe that witch will finally stop terrorizing children now.

⌘

On the way to lunch after Earth Science, everyone from class is still talking about how I stood up to Hailey last period. I smile to myself at first, but the more I hear about it, the more unsettled I become.

After finishing my chicken filet sandwich (one of the first appetizing school lunches of my freshman year, by the way), I decide to text Brett since I know he has a weight lifting class this period, and his teacher doesn't care if they text during class.

Riley: Hey! What're you up to?

Brett: Nothing much class is kinda boring right now. U?

Riley: Eating lunch. I just wanted to let you know that Hailey Carson the cheerleader is gonna try to ask you out. Haha I've been getting a good laugh out of it.

Brett: Really? Why's that funny?

Riley: Because she's so desperate haha

Brett: She is? That's pretty cool actually

Wait, what? I need some clarification here.

Riley: Cool? I thought we had a thing together?

Brett: Huh?

My throat goes dry as his message appears on my screen. How can he possibly not know what I'm talking about?

Riley: Didn't you take me on a date to the movies? You've been holding my hand. Texting me all the time. Telling me I'm beautiful. What else would I think?

Brett: Come on that was harmless flirting. I didn't mean it like that.

My stomach stings reading his admittance, as if a torpedo had been shot into it, knocking the breath out of me.

Can't Beat the Heart of a Carolina Girl

Why on earth would he go to the lengths to do all those sweet things and not mean it?

Riley: How could you do that to me? And you're willing to jump at a chance with her just like that?

Brett: Hey I'm just being honest. Yeah why not?

Honestly, I don't know why I'm still making an effort to text this jerk, but I feel the need to make a case.

Riley: Well she's horrible.

Brett: Hot though

He's got to be kidding me.

Riley: Seriously? That's all you care about?

Brett: What's your problem? U sound jealous.

Here it goes. It's not like I have any more dignity left to lose anyway.

Riley: Well I wonder why. I was being honest with you when I said I've liked you all this time.

Brett: I thought we were friends. I never wanted to be more than that.

Riley: Well I did but it doesn't matter anymore. I'm done with you.

Throwing my phone into my purse, I realize how naïve I've been the last three months, thinking that he actually wanted to date me. Now I regret even being friends with him. What, has my intuition decided to go work for Hailey too? Tears demand to be released from the crest of my eyes. I can't sit here in the middle of the cafeteria and bawl my eyes out, so I grab up my belongings, retreating outside before anyone can see me cry.

Sitting on the steps that lead to the walkway in front of the lunchroom, I investigate my bookbag, seizing some of the poems I had written about Brett inspired by our walks together and his sweet words, along with the copy of "Blue Eyes" I turned in for English. I reread it, realizing that after all my pining and daydreams involving him, Brett's nothing like the guy in the poem. Balling up the piece of paper, I hurl it into a nearby row of bushes, praying that the passage of time will weather the paper, as he has weathered my heart. With the release of the poem, the dam containing my tears finally collapses.

Seconds later, I hear the cafeteria door squeak open, though I refrain from looking up to see who it is. It's probably someone else that won't take the time of day to care, just like everyone else I know.

"Riley, there you are! I saw you leave the lunchroom. What's wrong?" a familiar, though soothing voice says from behind me. I peer over my shoulder hesitantly, not wanting to talk to anyone. There stands a boy in a red flannel shirt, donning a sympathetic expression. Guess who? Of course, Carter.

I wipe a few tears away from my cheeks, hating that he's seeing me in such a pathetic state. "Oh, hey Carter. Nothing's wrong; I just wanted to sit out here for a while."

Carter shakes his head, able to see through my guise. "Riley, you don't have to pretend for me; I know about the whole Brett situation," he admits, appearing crestfallen himself. "I see you walking with him every morning. Anyone with half a brain can tell how much you care about him. I'm just sorry he can't see it himself."

Though I'm still fighting back tears, this produces a weak smile. "Thanks, Carter. That's sweet."

"Oh, it's no problem. The main thing is I wanted to make sure you're okay. That idiot had no right to lead you on like that."

He manages to get a laugh from me. "Idiot doesn't cut it. He rejected someone who cares about him for Hailey, of all people."

Carter lets out a snicker, joining me on the step. "I can't stand Hailey either. I know we're not supposed to hate people, but she's a close exception."

"Why's that?"

"You know, obvious reasons. She's spoiled, skanky, and the worst thing… she's mean to you." He places his hand on my shoulder. "And that's a good enough reason to hate anybody."

Hearing someone knocking on the cafeteria window, Carter and I turn around to see Trent peering out at us from his seat. A sly grin crosses his face as his lips form the word, "Finally."

Chapter Eight

Entering third period the next day feels akin to stepping into my own grave. Though most people greet me with grins, remembering my epic outburst yesterday, Hailey titters from the back of the room, immediately bragging after catching my eye. "Look what Brettie just sent me! 'Good morning, gorgeous!' Isn't he the sweetest? I swear, I think I'm in love!"

"You've literally been dating for two hours," I sneer under my breath, throwing my bookbag down upon reaching my desk. Checking the time on my phone, I realize I've got another ninety-five minutes of torture to get through, being that class hasn't started yet and we have Mrs. Carothers as a sub again.

"Hey, how're you holding up?" Carter approaches my desk, breaking my train of thought. He takes a seat at the desk in front of me, as the girl who usually sits there has taken off early for Thanksgiving break.

"I've been better," I admit, gesturing to Hailey flaunting her messages.

"Let me guess, love at first emoticon?"

"How'd you know?"

"I've got skills. Well, not relationship skills, but skills nonetheless." He smolders awkwardly, cracking his knuckles in an attempt to pull off a James Dean vibe.

"Skills huh? As in burping the chorus of 'Sweet Home Alabama' skills, or binge watching all three *Lord of the Rings* in one sitting skills?" Trent questions, ruffling his friend's hair before taking a seat.

Carter's facial expression is priceless, appearing like a disgruntled puppy after its owner scolded him for peeing on the rug. "Will you please?"

Trent turns to me with a saddened disposition, motioning at Carter as if he's on display in an infomercial. "Will you please? Will you please, for the love of all that is holy, donate your affection to this poor, single soul? One date this year may just save his heart from the pain of rejection."

Though I try not to pan my eyes over to Carter, he looks as if he's about to explode in my peripheral vision. After his chivalrous act yesterday, I decide to jump to his rescue. "Right after Taylor donates to your fund."

"Donate to what fund?" Trent nearly jumps from his seat at the sound of Taylor's voice as she walks up from behind him.

"Keep on and I'll tell her!" I chime, eyeing my cousin daringly while nodding toward Carter.

"Touché," Trent rebuttals lowly.

Carter smiles softly at my gesture, mouthing "thank you". I wink, letting him know that Trent's comment doesn't bother me. For a moment, he looks as if he wants to add something more, before quickly averting his eyes again. I'm amazed by the fact that he's under this much pressure just talking to me. *No,* I think, *thank you, Carter.* Thank you for showing me what I should've been looking for the entire time.

⌘

This afternoon as I wait outside for Momma to come pick me up from school, Lexie and I talk about her experiences at Linwood Whaley High so far, our former friendship picking right back up from where we left off years ago.

"Again, I'm so sorry I didn't get a chance to say goodbye. Mom was desperate for work at the time since Daddy had just passed, and the company needed her immediately. So much for that job, though"—she rolls her eyes—"she lost her position when the offices moved to San Antonio."

"It's no problem." I laugh, noting that Lexie is just as chatty as she was when we were kids. "So did y'all move back because of that?"

"Nah, my stepdad wanted to move us closer to home. He's the greatest guy, Riles. He even adopted me as his own when he married Mom."

"So that's why you're a Thomas now! That's awesome, Lex."

"Yeah, and thanks for not asking me if I had gotten married. You can't imagine how many people have asked me that. People are so dumb."

"Now that you mention that, have you met any guys you like yet?" I prod. As the question leaves my lips, Brett rounds the corner. "But, if it's *that* guy, I wouldn't even bother. For the love of love itself, just run while you can!" Brett doesn't even bother to look at me as he walks by, further lighting my fury. I can be mad at him all I want, and I have the right.

"Dang Riley, harsh much? I haven't seen you this mad since Remy broke your Barbie doll back in second grade!"

I reminisce back to my—at the time four-year-old sister—sneaking into my room one night while Lexie was over and accidentally breaking one of the arms off my teenage Barbie doll. "Oh, it's worse than that! He led me on with all this sweet talk day after day, and then out of nowhere agrees to go out with a girl he's never even talked to, just because he thinks she's hot!" I scowl, not bothering to hide my frustration.

"Crush Hoarding Carson again?" Lexie acknowledges. She knows me so well, and how Hailey stole her crush in third grade.

"Yeah, that evil turd."

"Do you like anyone else? Maybe you could make him jealous by going out with another guy," she suggests.

"Nah, I'm not the kind to do that. And besides, why would I want his skank-loving self now?"

"Valid point."

"But, there is one guy I've talked to…" I admit cautiously.

"Wow, you talked to someone? That is a big deal!" Lexie snickers, picking on my introvert ways. When she realizes that I'm serious, she presses on, "How do you feel about him?"

I reflect on my conversations with Carter. He's been so sweet from the beginning. It's no secret that he had written that poem about his feelings for me. Plus, he stood by my side yesterday when it felt as if my heart would cease to be in a functional state again, all because of Brett. How could I have been so clueless? Carter's the one who cares about me, while Brett probably wouldn't care if I died for him.

"Riley, I repeat, do you like him?" Lexie shakes my shoulders, anxious for an answer.

"I think I just might," I conclude softly.

"Well, who is this fellow, young Riles?"

As if on cue, Carter, the guy I never thought I would reciprocate feelings for, exits the school and makes his way toward us. My eyes pace the ground as I hear the sound of footsteps approaching.

"Hot dang," Lexie realizes.

"Hey, Riley! Hi, hmm... you must be Lexie, right? You're new here?" he surmises, waving at the two of us.

"Sure am! And I don't know what your name is, but Riley was just telling me about you, and that, sir, is a big whoop," Lexie remarks, causing me to elbow her to stop.

"Oh, she was? That's cool," Carter says shyly, failing to hide his grin. "Y'all must've known each other before you moved here?"

"Yeah, we did. Well, she moved away, and then she came back. We're best friends," I blurt, instantly hating my own guts.

Lexie chuckles at my expense. "Yeah, ever since pre-school. She hasn't changed a bit."

Carter's mom pulls up in the parking lot, beeping the horn and waving as she does so. Carter squints in embarrassment and proceeds to walk toward the car. Turning around before he opens the passenger's side door, he calls, "See you after Thanksgiving, Riley!"

"Okay, see you!" I return, watching the car until it leaves the campus. "That's Carter Pickett," I explain, beaming like the sun on the fourth of July.

"He seems really nice Riley; why on earth wasn't he your first choice?" Lexie approves. "And besides, Mrs. Riley Addison Pickett sounds adorable!"

"Yeah, it does!" I agree, smiling wistfully before acknowledging how insane we sound, "but one step at a time, Lex." Momma pulls up seconds later, and I give Lexie a quick hug before leaving. This week has gone from good to horrendous, and now amazing. Now that I've realized how terrible my former judgments were, I'm confident that God's now writing an even better chapter for me.

⌘

Bolting straight to my room after I return home from school this afternoon, I write about the major events of this week in my diary. I barely know where to start; to tell the truth, this has been one of the most action-packed weeks of my life. Lexie moving back is pretty incredible, though, so I begin with that.

After I compose a three-page entry about these pre-Thanksgiving miracles, I lie down on my bed, considering Brett's choice. He's making a huge mistake dating Hailey, but I guess that's what he deserves if the sole thing he looks for in a girl consists of everything but honorable qualities.

Gagging at the thought, my cell phone starts to ring, the ringtone being "Breakaway" by Kelly Clarkson. "Hey Taylor, what's up?" I answer, not even bothering to check the caller ID.

"I didn't want to ask about it in science, but I heard that Brett and Hailey are dating now. I could barf. I'm so sorry, Riles."

"Oh, it's nothing. I talked to him and he only likes her because he thinks she's hot. I thought he was smarter than that, but guess what I learned?"

"What?"

"We were so wrong yesterday; Brett's definitely in her league. Both of them are just superficial, spoiled brats."

"Glad to see you haven't lost your sense of humor over the situation, Riles." Taylor laughs. "Well, I've gotta go. See you at school!"

"Okay, see you!" I hang up, flopping back on my bed as I do so. I can't think of anything else to do, except for watching *The Lizzie McGuire Movie*, the most cherished movie from my childhood. Loading the DVD on my laptop, I round up some snacks and Dr. Pepper, pretending I'm Lizzie and that Carter is my secret knight in shining armor, Gordo, until the ending credits roll. I know, corny right? Well, please excuse me for not caring. I'm just glad that I may now have a chance of actually dating a guy who'll appreciate me.

Chapter Nine

On Monday, I return to school after our weeklong Thanksgiving break. Lexie was able to spend the night on Friday, Momma's side of the family came over and ate Thanksgiving dinner with us, and I watched reruns of *Reba* and *Full House*. Nowhere near intriguing, I know. But, I am Riley Houston. What did you expect?

The morning announcements consist of congratulating Brett on scoring the winning touchdown in the last game of the season (yawn), announcing that someone needs to return Joel's stolen gym clothes, and that the Black and White Ball is coming up. The crown jewel of dances at Linwood Whaley High, the Black and White Ball is revered more than homecoming and is decorated more lavishly than prom. It's the biggest dance of the year, and yes, I'm going. It'll be the first dance I've ever attended, but it'll be worth it if I get to dance with Carter.

First period dragged by because the teacher went into a full-on lecture about the importance of resume building. Second period was fun, being that Lexie and I watched videos on YouTube while Ms. Mitchell went to assist another teacher with a problem about an overhead projector. In third period we actually learned about science for once, but by mid-class

Mr. Donoghue had to run an errand (go to McDonald's), so we've been shooting the breeze ever since.

"So, are you still okay about the whole Brett thing?" Taylor asks, looking up from the English notes she's been studying.

I'm not listening, for daydreams of Carter and me at the Black and White Ball are rolling through my mind, a smile donning my face.

"Apparently!" Taylor acknowledges, giggling to herself. "Hey Riley, guess what? I'm marrying this hobo I met the other day. He only has one tooth, but it shines so brightly!"

"Oh, that's nice..." I respond, not paying a lick of attention. Carter's so shy; I wonder if he'll even work up the courage to ask me to dance. The thought crosses my mind that maybe I should ask him. I grimace, knowing that this whole escapade is going to be harder than I imagined. I mean, what if neither one of us—

"Riley, there's a lizard on you!" Taylor tries again, full of enthusiasm.

"What? Where?!" I shriek, almost falling out of my chair.

Trent practically loses it. "What's the matter with you?"

"Like you don't know!" I shoot back, full of sarcasm.

"What did I do?" Trent asks, the picture of innocence. He obviously has no idea that his schemes have placed me under a crush spell. Carter glances up from a copy of *Fellowship of the Ring* to see what's going on.

The fact that he's watching me from across the room sends me into panic mode. "Um… you know, bring lizards in here. You still play with them, right?"

"Not since that last one peed on me," he admits downheartedly.

Taylor's face contorts in repulsion. "You let it pee on you?"

"No. I let it bite my ear and hang there like an earring. Then when I wasn't paying attention, it peed. All over me."

"Nice to know, Trent…" Taylor acknowledges slowly, turning back to her notes.

Carter gets up from his desk and joins our conversation. "Has he always been like that? Like I can't imagine him as a toddler."

"Pretty much," I snicker, a smile playing across my lips.

Trent casts us a look of disdain. "Alright, y'all be that way! I got you two together, and now you're making fun of me? That's the kind of thanks I get?"

"Oh snap, what is this I hear?" Taylor questions, not hiding her surprise.

From the corner of my eye, I peek at Carter. His face has flushed blood red. I know mine will be the same, as my cheeks are growing warmer by the second. "No," I mutter.

"We're not together," Carter adds. Almost as if he's attempting to contradict his words, he meets my eyes. It's not your ordinary look either; his gaze lingers too long, the corners of his mouth have turned up slightly, despite himself. For the first time in my life, there's no guesswork involved with this crush. But then again, we're both too shy to let the other know, and the silence is deafening.

"Then what was that?" Trent proposes, referring to the moment Carter and I just shared.

"What, I can't look at Riley? Gosh Trent, you sure are protective of your cousin!" Carter defends, turning his attention to the watch on his wrist, which coincidentally needs his immediate attention for adjustment.

"Carter, don't push me dude," Trent remarks, pressing a no-nonsense look. "I know how you feel about Riley."

Carter's face remains red. "Trent, Riley's a good friend... we're just friends."

He glimpses at me again, signaling for help, and I follow his lead, ready to pull out my threat from our last class meeting. "Yeah, we're just friends. Trent, did you ever tell Taylor about your crush on her in the fifth grade?" This is my lovely attempt to change the subject.

Trent's face distorts in shock, and Carter and I can barely help but laugh. "Um, no, but that was four years ago!" Trent snaps, defending himself.

"Oh, it's okay. I kinda had a crush on you then, too, but now I regret it. Especially since you still play with lizards!" Taylor jokes. Trent scrubs her head playfully, messing up her hair.

"Aw, they're in love!" Carter remarks lightheartedly.

"Shut up, Carter!" they utter simultaneously.

"Well, I would go on back to my seat since y'all are so mean," Carter continues, placing his hands on the back of my chair, "but I don't wanna leave poor Riley alone with you two lunatics!"

"Oh yeah, because 'friends' don't leave 'friends' alone with crazy people… who are actually your own friends. Yeah, that makes total sense," Trent rambles.

I slap my hand over my cousin's mouth, tired of his accusations, as truthful as they are. Carter and I may be "just friends" right now, but our story is on the verge of beginning. But, then again, when will that day come? Hopefully sooner than I think.

⌘

Allyson Kennedy

December 10, 2008

Dear Diary,

The Black and White Ball is this Saturday, and I still haven't found a dress to wear. I want to look amazing because yesterday Trent said that Carter is planning on going. I talked to him yesterday in class. I'm glad we're friends now; too bad that couldn't have happened sooner.

Saying that I'm anxious for the dance is an understatement. Despite being ecstatic over the fact that Carter is going, there's still the haunting fact that I've never been to a dance before, and am as coordinated as a newborn calf when I'm walking in heels. In middle school, school dances were never the place for a loner like me; I opted to spend each one at home, snuggled up to my GameCube playing *Animal Crossing* instead. Only people with an actual social life ever dared to go. But this year, I'm determined to change that. I'm going to show them that I, Riley Houston, am worth noticing, and that Brett should have realized it before Hailey ever sauntered into the picture.

As I walk downstairs to ask Momma if we can go dress shopping before Saturday, the doorbell chimes. Opening the front door, I find Trent's older sister, Grace, and her two-year-old son, Rylan.

"Grace! How've you been?" I ask in excitement, as she sets Rylan down before reaching out to me for a hug. Rylan runs into the living room, standing in awe as he finds *SpongeBob SquarePants* playing on the television.

"B-Bob, Mommy! B-Bob!" he squeals, pointing at the screen.

"Pretty good, Riles! I wish I could come visit more, but Isaac and I have been so busy with adulthood and all that. I'm glad you're home, though," Grace says, pulling a clothing bag from behind her back. "I have something for you."

She hands me the bag, explaining as I unzip it, "Word got back to me through Aunt Joyce that you're going to your first dance this weekend." I nod, confirming what I know she's heard through the family grapevine. "And you haven't even got your dress?"

I know why she's here now. "Grace, you didn't!"

"Go ahead and see what's in the bag," she encourages. I remove the bag from the hanger, revealing the most beautiful dress I've ever laid eyes on. Made from a flowy black material, it includes a white trim around the waist. The trim ties in the back, while the front features a square, silver stone-covered accent.

"This is perfect," I sigh, already trying to imagine how Carter will react to seeing me in this. "Thank you so much!"

"Oh, it was nothing; it was so easy to make," Grace adds modestly.

"You made this?" It looks as if it could have come straight from a department store. But, giving Grace some credit, she's always been amazing at making clothes.

"Yep! Actually, I made it a couple months ago to give you as a Christmas present, but I felt that you needed it now." Smiling with enthusiasm, she winks. "Especially since my little bro likes to play matchmaker! Plus, I still feel like I need to offer you some kind of compensation for that hack job haircut I gave you."

Laughing, I add, "Don't worry about it; it grew back just fine!"

"Mommy! B-Bob went bye-bye!" Rylan interjects, crossing his arms and poking out his lip as the cartoon comes to an end.

"Aw, Rylan come here," I coax, scooping him up as he runs into my arms.

"Riwey!" he gushes, resting his soft little head on my shoulder.

"Rylan, you sure are growing up!" I say, kissing his forehead as I struggle to hold him.

Grace reaches for him, laughing. "He's getting to be a big boy now. I think he takes after his Uncle Trent in that regard. We think he's gonna be a football player when he gets older. Well, we better be getting on. I have to cook supper. Rylan wants tacos," she explains, hugging me goodbye.

"I wove tacos!" Rylan giggles, reaching out of his mother's arms to hug me.

"You're so sweet!" I laugh, tapping his cute button nose.

After their departure, I'm left alone in the house with the TV on and nothing else to do. Might as well watch a Christmas movie, I decide, heading toward the movie stash in the hallway closet.

"Let's see, what do we have?" I ask myself, skimming over the DVD titles. Most of our movies are cartoons because my sister's only ten. Luckily for me, I stumble across one of my favorites, from Hallmark. "Hmm… there's nothing wrong with watching this for the fiftieth time." I grin, pulling *The Christmas Card* off the shelf.

Walking back into the living room, I place the disk in the DVD player before settling deep into my favorite chair: the worn-out green recliner in the corner. Momma wants to get rid of this thing so bad, but I won't let her. Nobody's getting rid of my favorite chair!

Navigating through the disk's menu, my mind keeps wondering what will be in store for this weekend. What if

Carter decides not to show up? What if Hailey and Brett find a way to embarrass me? Hopefully, nothing like that will occur, or at least I hope not.

Chapter Ten

Well, tonight's set to be the most fabulous night my fourteen-year-old self has ever anticipated: Linwood Whaley High's annual Black and White Ball. I'm preparing to be star-studded, though I'm not ready for the divas (the Preps, if you're wondering), or the fact that there might be a romantic scene up ahead that all the hopeless crushing I've done in my lifetime has anything but prepared me for. Nevertheless, I'm ready to hit the red carpet for the first time, even if it is just the crusty welcome mat in the cafeteria.

Getting ready has already proved to be a pain and a half. My hair won't do right every way that I've tried styling it, but eventually I get it to stay with a little hairspray. Makeup's a breeze, though I've never been known to wear much anyway. Just a little foundation, blush, and mascara completes my routine. Well, except for the neutral eyeshadow I add, just for the special occasion.

Tossing my hair back, I stand in front of the bathroom mirror to look myself over. I can't help but gaze at my reflection in amazement. My golden blonde hair drapes long off my shoulders, luminous in a way it has never appeared before.

"You look gorgeous, Shug." I hear someone say from behind me. In the mirror's reflection, I see Momma standing at the door.

A soft smile emerges, which I hide by smoothing out a wrinkle in the skirt. That's something I don't get called often. "Thanks, Momma," I answer back, noticing that she's holding something behind her back. "What's that?"

She pulls out a shiny, black clutch bag. "Something to keep your money in for the dance," she laughs. "What did you think it was, a puppy?"

Rolling my eyes in mock anger, I take the bag from her, sticking the five dollars she had given me earlier for the cover fee in there. "You're so hilarious, Momma," I mumble, countering her sarcasm. From there, I exit the bathroom and grab my cell phone from the end table in the living room.

"Is your phone charged up?" Momma asks, peering over my shoulder as I check for any messages from Lexie or Taylor.

"Yes, Momma."

"Are you sure?" she continues, walking into the laundry room.

"Yes, I'm sure."

"Riley, you know I can't hear you from in here!"

"It finished charging an hour ago!" I repeat for the third time, growing slightly irritated.

"Okay then," she replies, walking back out of the laundry room. She glances at the clock. "It's seven-thirty. Are you ready for me to drop you off?"

I swallow, attempting to rid my nerves. "Sure, let's go."

⌘

"Bye!" I tell Momma, as I pull the door to her Pacifica closed. Walking down the breezeway, I search for Lexie and Taylor, as we've planned to walk in together.

"Hey Riley, over here!" I hear Taylor call from the bushes near the cafeteria, our designated meeting place.

"Hey y'all!" I reply as I walk over, nearly tripping in my heels.

Lexie snorts. "Still haven't gotten used to those, have you?"

"Nope. I kind of like them, though, but they're nothing compared to my Rainbows." I smile, shifting my feet in the black, strappy heels.

"God sure did bless that guy with a nice everything!" Taylor babbles, staring at Will Shepard as he walks past us to the cafeteria-turned-ballroom.

"Why don't you go talk to him?" I suggest, laughing at her expense.

"You know dang well I can't," she complains, still staring. "My goodness, just look at the perfection that is Will Shepard."

"Oh well, he'll be the next one to go out with Tiffany then. You know he's friends with Brett the Terrible, right?" I muse aimlessly, sending a humorous wink Lexie's way.

"Well, okay, when you put it that way, let's go!" Taylor springs into action, nearly sprinting down the breezeway with Lexie and myself hurrying behind her.

I'm the last one of my friends to make it to the door, note the heels I'm now regretting. Not many people are here yet, but I spy Trent standing near the snack table (where else would he be?) so I decide to go bug him.

"Hey Trent, what's up?"

He gives me a blank stare for a second, until he finally asks, almost incredulous, "Riley, is that you?" He squints at me hard, as if I'm a combination of every math problem he's ever faced.

"Yeah Cuz, it's me," I respond, grabbing a cookie from the snack table. "Why?"

"Well, I didn't recognize you!" He peers down at me again. "And I don't think I've ever seen you in a dress, either."

"I just wore a dress to church last Sunday!"

"You did? Well, I don't remember!"

"That's because you fell asleep halfway through the sermon." I laugh, recalling the dirty glance one of the deacons kept shooting his way while he was nodding off.

"Oh yeah…" Trent chuckles, shoving his hands into his pockets. The cafeteria door opens, peaking his interest. Guess who?

"Hey look, there's Carter! Yo Fartblossom, over here!" Trent yells, waving at his friend. Checking my reaction, he snickers as I produce a weak smile. "I knew it!"

"What?" I question, feigning disinterest.

"Someone's finally fallen for her Gordo!" Trent sings, obviously amused.

"C-Carter?" I stutter, hating that I can't speak to defend myself. "We're friends I guess, but—"

"Yeah Riley, save it. I'm about to do you a huge favor," Trent cuts me off. Carter arrives in front of us seconds later.

"Hey y'all." Carter waves shyly, rubbing the back of his neck.

Trent looks at Carter and then back to me, a mischievous gleam in his eyes. "Well Riley, Carter sure does clean up good, doesn't he?"

With this excuse, I finally allow myself to take a good gander at Carter. He has on a black tux, shiny black shoes, and he smells like Heaven. I have no clue, of course, if Heaven even has a scent, but if it does, it'd be just as amazing. "Yeah, he does," I manage, avoiding eye contact out of fear.

Trent grins from ear to ear, patting my shoulder. "You don't look too bad either, Riley. Right, Carter?"

Glancing back up to catch his reaction, I see Carter blushing like crazy. "She's beautiful, as always," he admits, shuffling his feet.

Suddenly, Carter and I duck in cover as a plastic spoon catapults over the snack table, smacking Trent in the forehead. "Ow! Who threw that?!" he scowls. Over on the other side of the room, I can see Taylor is trying to call him over. "Oh, it's you," he yells back, rolling his eyes. "Taylor probably wants to dance with me. Her and every other girl out there," he comments to us as he slicks back his hair and walks away.

So here I am, left alone with Carter. Racking my brain, I desperately search for something to say to keep us here together. Allowing myself another peek in his direction, his entire face is still burning red with embarrassment. Mine probably is, too, but I have to say something. This is the chance I've been waiting for since my realization, and I'm not about to lose it like I lost my chance with Brett, if you even called that a chance.

"So… do you think Trent is really gonna dance with Taylor?" I begin bashfully, clearing my throat.

He smiles, examining them from where we're standing. "Well, I don't know. They're arguing right now." He laughs, pointing.

I catch sight of them, Trent gabbing on about something, giggling to himself, and Taylor with her brow furrowed, looking as if she could kill him. "I hope they will soon enough. That would be adorable."

"Yeah, they'd make a cute couple," Carter agrees warily, as Taylor takes a swing at Trent for messing with her hair. "If they don't murder one another first, that is."

"What do you think they're talking about?" I wince as Taylor snarls at Trent, snatching a barrette back from his clutches.

"I have no idea," Carter ponders, "but if I had to guess…"

"Duh, I know that, Smart-Fart," Trent yells at Taylor after an obnoxiously loud rap song ends, unaware that we can hear him. "They're not dancing because all they're playing is rap! I know Carter. The kid has no swag. But, he loves country."

94

Carter facepalms himself. "Apparently my lack of dance skills."

"I thought you said you had skills?" I ask, amused.

"Not those kind of skills either, if I'm being honest."

"Me neither." I laugh, loving that I can be myself around him. "I took dance classes when I was younger and that was an epic fail if there ever was one. Wait, what are they doing now?" I nudge Carter, pointing to Taylor on the other side of the room, who's digging in her purse and handing her pink iPod Nano over to Trent. From what I can tell, it seems as if they're discussing songs.

"Really? Because I think they'd like 'Chicken Fried'," Trent suggests, his voice growing louder.

Taylor grabs his shirt collar, growing hostile. "No! They need a romantic song, not one about chicken and beer! Gosh, just give it back, I'll go do it! Call Carter and tell him to ask her to dance when it starts playing." She snatches her iPod back and runs off to the DJ.

"Being anything but inconspicuous," Carter answers at last, laughing nonetheless.

⌘

Can't Beat the Heart of a Carolina Girl

As Carter and I are still making awkward small talk about the possible romantic comedy that is Trent and Taylor, Carter's phone begins to ring.

"Excuse me," he apologizes, pulling out his Razor V1 with a camouflage cover on it. "Hello?" he answers in an annoyed tone.

"Carter, this is it bud!" Trent practically yells into the phone. Looking around to see where he is, I finally locate him staring at us from outside one of the cafeteria windows… literally five feet away from where we're standing. I have to bite my tongue to keep from laughing.

Carter winces in pain from the shout and lowers his tone. "What are you talking about? Why did you stop me from talking to Riley?" He glances back over at me, grimacing because I overheard him.

"I just wanted to tell you to ask her to dance when the next song comes on," Trent explains, motioning through the window to Taylor, who has just handed over her iPod.

"But what if I mess it up? She probably doesn't like me anyway," Carter admits with crestfallen spirit, thinking the music is drowning him out. His eyes shift in my direction again, beautiful as ever.

Trent sighs in frustration at the end of the line, though I'm unable to read his lips through the window this time. He seems to be laying a life lesson on Carter, as he looks like his dad whenever he's lecturing Trent about doing his homework.

Whatever he said, it causes Carter to turn to me with a bright smile, and I return it, though I'm a bit confused. "Alright, I'm going for it. Wish me luck!" He places his phone into his tux pocket and informs me, "That was Trent." I nod, pointing to the window behind me. His blue eyes practically bulge out of their sockets at the knowledge that I had found the hidden location of his wingman. To his luck, "Lord Knows" begins to play over the speakers.

"Oh, I love this song!" I exclaim. "This has been one of my favorites since I was little."

"That's good," Carter replies smoothly at first, though his confidence falters soon after. "So I guess you wouldn't mind if..." Our eyes meet, not allowing him to finish his sentence.

Somehow I summon the courage, so I continue for him, "If we danced together?" Carter grins, leading me out to the dance floor.

I thought I had been nervous *before* coming to the dance. Now, I'm practically shaking. But, as Carter slips his arms around me, it all seems to fade away. I'm immediately caught up in the chorus:

"You heard me when I was silent.

You took a chance, knowing I was blinded.

Out of circumstance, into something new.

Lord knows how much I needed you."

Gazing into Carter's breathtaking blue eyes, I can now say I've witnessed a miracle. His eyes contain the brightest sense of hope, hope that I have never before encountered in the dark and ludicrous eyes of Brett Harvey. Brett's now on the bottom of the totem pole of guys I would ever consider in my future; yet when I consider Carter, I know that my life will only be better with him in it, for he somehow sees the promise in me that no one has yet to see. Something has to happen between us before it's too late.

"Riley, can I tell you something?" Carter asks nervously.

"Yeah, anything," I answer breathlessly, emerging from my thoughts.

"Well, I know we've just recently started becoming friends and all, but I've had this amazing feeling about you since the first time I saw you." He practically blurts the sentence out, his face instantly enveloped in crimson, matching the Christmas bows tied to the doors of the cafeteria.

Without the slightest hesitation, I react by reaching over and kissing his cheek, surprising myself in the process. His eyes bolt up suddenly, beaming. "I hope that means you feel the same way!"

"Don't worry, it does." A small smile creeps onto my face as I watch him look at me that way.

"I know it's sudden and everything, but I've never felt this way about anyone else before, and it's been killing me that you're not with me," Carter confesses. "So, would you do me the honor of allowing me to be your boyfriend?"

"Of course, Carter," I gush, combating my shaking knees.

Carter immediately pulls me into a hug. "I'm so glad this finally happened."

Jolting us back to reality, someone hollers out, "Yes!" Carter and I leap apart, finding Trent and Taylor leaned up against the snack table like a couple stalkers behind us.

"Trent Liam Houston, what are you doing?" I interrogate, caught off-guard by the sudden appearance of our friends.

"Dancing. What are you doing?" Trent counters in the same questionable tone as he busts out a disco move. "Dancing with your new beau?"

Turning back around, I grin at Carter. "Why, yes I am! And you're dancing with my friend?" Trent freezes on the spot, a freaked out expression on his face.

"Either you were dancing with her or spying on us, Trent *Liam*," Carter urges, snickering as he says Trent's middle name.

Trent stares at us, narrow-eyed. "Fine. We were spying on you."

Taylor glances up at him, mumbling, "Dang, you could have lied!"

Trent shoots her a bewildered look. "You wanted them to think we danced together?"

"No," Taylor huffs, blowing her side bangs out of her eyes. "It just would've made it less obvious that we were spying on them."

"I think you two should dance. Y'all would make a cute little couple. About like those two in *You've Got Mail*," Carter comments jokingly.

"Shut up, Carter!" they retort in unison.

Over our amusing accusations, another, though drastically more annoying voice arises. "Oh Brett, magenta looks so adorbs on you!" Hailey giggles, leaning in to kiss him.

Brett leans back to avoid it. "You know, Hailey, pink ain't really my color. I'm more of a Carolina blue guy. And besides, this is the Black and White Ball, not a Victoria's Secret prom."

"But Brettie, I like totally *love* pink! You don't want to disappoint me, do you? Besides, blue is so *icky*!" Brett rolls his eyes at her comment and continues to dance.

100

Shaking my head, I direct my attention back to Carter. "You would've let him wear anything he wanted, wouldn't you?" Carter solicits knowingly.

"Yeah, but he blew the chance." I take his hand, cradling it in both of mine. "And I pray you won't."

Running his thumb over the back of my hand, Carter can't suppress a grin from forming. "I'd never blow the chance I've waited my entire life to take."

The lights in the cafeteria turn on, signaling everyone that it's time to go. Pulling Carter in for one last hug, I whisper, "Well, I hope to make it worth the wait." As I walk to the parking lot, I can't help but feel as if a fireworks show is sparkling off inside of me.

⌘

When Momma arrives to pick me up from the dance, she can't help but notice the permanent grin that has settled onto my face as I hop into the passenger's seat. "Since when do you smile that much?"

"Well, let's just say it's been a pretty dang good night!" I laugh, trying and failing to stop smiling as I reach down to buckle my seatbelt.

"Oh gosh, don't tell me. You danced with Brett, didn't you?" my little sister, Remy, protests from the back seat.

Turning around to answer her, my face contorts with disgust. "Eww, no! I danced with my boyfriend," I answer, full of pride.

Both Momma and Remy look at me as if I'm speaking Chinese. "Since when do you have a boyfriend, Miss Ma'am?" Remy inquires, poking her head in-between the front two seats.

"Since tonight, if you must know. His name's Carter, and now I can say I date the sweetest guy in the world." I relish the words leaving my lips as I sink down in my seat.

Momma glances over at me curiously, suppressing a somewhat nervous laugh. "So, where did you two lovebirds meet?"

"Trent introduced us on the first day of school. I don't think I've ever appreciated him more in my life."

"You met through Trent?" Remy cackles. "Good luck with that!"

Turning around to face her squarely, I'm quick to defend Trent's matchmaking skills. "He happens to be quite the gentleman. A heck of a lot nicer than Brett's ever been."

"Well, I could've told you Brett was a butt. Wait, I did! But you never listened to me, did you? You just *had* to fall for him! Sitting around all the dang time waiting on that wannabe

Matthew McConaughey…" Remy rambles, waving her arms around for emphasis.

Momma catches sight of her in the rearview mirror and smiles. "It'll be funny one day when she ends up doing the same thing," she whispers to me. "I'm just glad you're happy with someone, Riley, as long as he's not a delinquent or a creepy stalker."

I laugh. "Don't worry, Momma. He's just sweet Carter Pickett."

As soon as we park in the garage, I walk in the house and pull off those heels that have been killing me since I first arrived at Linwood Whaley High tonight. Daddy sees me walking through the hallway and has to ask to take pictures. As tired as I am, I begrudgingly comply. I mean, a night as perfect as tonight deserves some photographic evidence, even if Carter's not here. So, after he takes twelve shots of me by the stairs, I retire to my room, change into pajamas, and write about the beginning of this new fairy tale in my diary, inspired by the fact that I've just scored my first prince at my first ball.

Chapter Eleven

Christmas break made its debut this week. I consider myself blessed that the semester ended the way it did: Carter and I getting together and Brett being miserable under Hailey's control. I still smirk at the thought, for he deserves every bit of annoyance she causes, and then some.

On the first day of break, Momma tells Remy and me to clean out our bookbags. My English binder has fallen apart over the semester; the front cover is barely hanging on as I pull it out of the main compartment. Mrs. Griffin had tortured us with all of that work, and when she said to take notes on something, it wasn't just a suggestion. Picking through my binder, I find a six-page series of notes I had taken on just one chapter of *The Odyssey*. My hands were cramped for a week after I wrote those, but it was worth it because I made a 97 on the final exam.

"Dang, English was the only hard class I had this semester," I surmise to Remy, who is trashing everything in sight.

Her eyes widen at all the paper I have spread out on the floor. "What did she try to do, kill y'all?"

"That's what Taylor and I thought at first, but Mrs. Griffin's nice. I guess all the work's for our own good, though.

Well, most of it." I glare down at a ten-page book report I had to do on *I Never Promised You a Rose Garden*. *That* I could have done without.

"My teachers are all nice, except for Ms. Doo. I can't stand her!" Remy mumbles, stuffing what looks like a geography project in the trash bag.

"Ms. Doo? Who the heck is she, Scooby's wife?"

"No, she's just this weird old lady that teaches my Social Studies class. She says she has thirteen poodles *in* her house."

"Point taken..."

"So, have you talked to Prince Charming since the Black and White Ball, Cinderella?" Remy asks jokingly.

"Yeah, on the phone this morning, Ugly Stepsister." Remy narrows her eyes, slapping my arm after the jab.

"Dang Remy, I was just kidding! Carter wants to take me out on our first official date tonight. I can't wait!"

"Do you know what you're going to wear yet?" Remy questions skeptically, running her eyes over my present outfit, which consists of black sweatpants and a Linwood Whaley High T-shirt.

"No, I mean I still have a few hours," I reply cautiously.

"Riley, what am I going to do with you? The first time a decent boy asks you on a date, and you haven't even got an outfit picked out? You're gonna blow it big time! You'll end up like Ms. Doo, a divorced old woman with a dog infestation and blue hair!"

"Thanks for making me feel real good about myself, Sis." I fail to hide my annoyance.

"Anytime. Now, to the closet! March up those stairs!"

This lecture is coming out of the mouth of my fashion-conscious ten-year-old sister. Won't she be pleasant when she's my age? I'm kinda glad I'll be off to college by then.

Pulling the door open to my closet, Remy instantly butts her head in to present herself with the options I have available. She runs her hand across a few of my long-sleeve shirts until she discovers the perfect one. "How about this?" She pulls down a periwinkle V-neck sweater. Skepticism rises for a second, but I decide that arguing with her may be a dangerous decision. We pair it with a white lace camisole, a pair of dark denim skinny jeans, and a pair of moccasins.

"Now that is being prepared for a date!" Remy smiles proudly, patting the pile of clothes.

I can't help but roll my eyes at my sister's forwardness. "Please child, you're ten. You've hardly even talked to a boy, let alone dated one."

"I talk to Ben, Brett's brother!" Remy whines, "That so counts!"

"Nope. People related to Brett Harvey do not count at all," I state curtly, plopping down on the beanbag in the corner.

"You're so weird, Riley," Remy refutes, exiting my room. Weird or not, I'm the one with the date coming up, and I'm darn proud that it's not with Brett.

⌘

"So that's two sweet teas, two barbecue sandwiches with no slaw, and two medium fries?" our waitress, Lola, reviews our order, smiling softly as she glances back up at Carter and me. For our first date, he decided to take me to his favorite restaurant in town, McKiver's Café, which also happens to be my favorite. To make it even funnier, we both share the same favorite meal from McKiver's, right down to discarding the perpetual nastiness that is coleslaw.

"That's perfect," Carter replies, the grin he's been donning since he (along with his daddy, who allowed Carter to drive with his learner's permit) first picked me up tonight.

"Alright, you two cuties, your food will be out in a bit!"

"You know what's weird?" I ask Carter as Lola is scurrying back to the kitchen.

"That I somehow talked you into going on a date with me?" Carter jokes, sticking his tongue out at me as he reaches for my hand.

"Oh goodness, no, you crazy thing." I smile, finding his self-deprecating wit amusing, especially for how cute he is. "I mean how we've both been eating at McKiver's since we were little and I've never once seen you in here."

"That's because you didn't know me," my boyfriend replies, stacking the pepper shaker on top of the salt shaker with his free hand. "You can see the same people around all the time and never know them. It's easy to overlook them like that. I've seen you in here with your family quite a few times, though."

This makes me smile, as I remember the information Trent relayed to me at Youth Group. "I'm sorry, Carter. I wish I could've remembered you from Trent's party. He told me about that, how you helped me up when I fell."

"Oh gosh, he told you all that?!" Carter winces, slapping his palm to his forehead. "Please tell me that was all he said?"

"Well..." I pause good-naturedly, relishing in the fact that he's still trying to make a good impression on me. "I don't want to start out our relationship by lying to you. He mentioned how you asked about me after the party, too—"

"Yeah, it's settled. I'm going to strangle him," he cuts me off, groaning into his hand, obviously humiliated. Lola comes back to the table with our teas, raising her eyebrows at Carter as she walks away.

"What? There's nothing wrong with that." I laugh, squeezing his hand. "How many guys do you think have ever gone out of their way to find out more about me? Zero. If anything, it's sweet, not whatever you're thinking."

He peeks through his fingers at me, those blue eyes sparkling with wonder. "You're serious?"

I nod my head, too caught up in the fact that this adorable guy in front of me cares this much about what I think of him.

"It's official, I have the best girlfriend ever!" He drops his hand, revealing a timid smile. "If I were you, I'd run for the hills if I heard that. I mean, I'm kind of relieved you don't remember me from back then. I was the biggest nerd in school."

"*You* were the biggest nerd? Did you not see me at that party?" I laugh. "Heck, that's probably why I don't remember you! I've tried to rid my mind of all things sixth grade."

"What, the cute, clumsy girl with short blonde hair who made some of the wittiest comments about Trent that I've ever heard? The one who smiled at me when I helped her up, revealing that a mouthful of braces can still look adorable?"

I lean back in the booth, incredulous. "You've got to be kidding."

"Does this look like the face of a kidder?" He points to his face, striking a deadpan expression. "I know you probably hated all of those things about yourself, but that day... wow, that day... you sure made a lasting impression on my heart. There's no other way to put it than that."

Twenty minutes into our date, and I'm already at a loss for words. But this time, wariness has not a thing to do with it.

⌘

"Bye Momma! Try not to eat all the fudge before I get back, Remy!" I say before stepping out of the car and walking up the steps of Carter's front porch. After we shared the first date of a lifetime, when Carter (yes, along with his driving aid) dropped me back off at my house that night, he immediately asked me to hang out again on Friday, tonight.

"I ain't making any promises!" Remy hollers, rolling up her window. I take in a nervous breath as I place my finger on the doorbell, praying that his family will like me. Two seconds later, Carter opens the door.

"Hey Riles, come on in!" he greets, taking my hand and leading me inside the house. The first thing to catch my eye is an enormous Christmas tree, decorated heavily with ornaments ranging from Hallmark collectibles to Ford trucks.

"Wow, your tree is beautiful!" I admire, failing to suppress a smile when I catch sight of an ornament that houses a picture of Carter as a toddler.

"Why thank you, Shug!" A woman in her early forties donning a baking apron and ginger hair enters the living room, beaming at us.

"Momma, this is Riley," Carter introduces lowly, embarrassed by his mother's obvious expression of enthusiasm.

"Oh Carter, she's even prettier than you said!" Mrs. Pickett exclaims, immediately pulling me into a hug.

"Aw, thanks," I answer from my squished position as I awkwardly pat her back, unsure of what to say.

Luckily, a timer chimes off in the kitchen. "Oh, that must be those peanut butter cookies!" She retreats back to her former occupation to attend to them, leaving us behind.

"Sorry about that. Momma's a hugger," Carter apologizes, running his hand over his face.

"Oh, she's fine, I'm used to it. My cousin Grace is the same way." I laugh. "I like your momma; she seems super nice."

Carter smiles slightly. "Well, I'm glad to hear that because she's been asking me all week when she's going to be able to meet you. She's a little jealous of Daddy since he got to see you the other day." Clearing his throat, he adds, "So, what

111

do you want to do? We can watch a movie or play a game, or..."

"Anything's fine Carter," I answer, liking his nervousness.

"Alright, let's ride the four wheeler then," he radiates, grabbing my hand.

He leads me outside, across the backyard to his daddy's shop, and hops onto the ATV. "You want to drive?" he proposes, patting the worn leather seat.

"Well, I've never driven one before. I've heard they can be dangerous," I explain, somewhat uncomfortable.

"Don't worry, I don't drive like a maniac. The path we're going on is clear, so we shouldn't have anything to worry about. I promise I won't let it do anything to hurt you," Carter replies innocently. The sincerity in his eyes is all the guarantee I need, so I give in.

"Alright, you've got me," I consent, taking a seat behind him.

"Okay, now just hold on to me," he instructs, handing me a helmet and slapping his own on his head. I slide my arms around him, and he pulls out of the shop.

"Daddy made me this track around the field when I was little," Carter explains as we begin down the dirt trail that runs along the edge of the barren field. "He used to live here when he was a kid, so he's shown me all the cool ins and outs

112

of the woods back here." Carter takes a right turn at an opening in the woods, leading onto another dirt path.

"It's so pretty back here!" I comment, taking in all of the fallen leaves that decorate the path.

"Yeah, you should see it in the peak of October. Maybe I can take you down here next year, *if* you can put up with me for that long." Carter smiles over his shoulder at me, causing me to wrinkle my nose playfully at his comment.

We've been riding for a while when we reach another opening. Turning left, a huge pond comes into view, surrounded by dozens of pine trees. Carter pulls the vehicle to a halt near one of the tallest trees. He unbuckles his helmet, setting it on the seat, and I follow suit. Jumping off the four-wheeler, he reaches into his pocket to pull out his pocket knife.

"What are you up to, Carter?" I ask, admiring the height of the trees surrounding us.

"Follow me over here and you'll see." His eyes glisten in the fading sunlight. I hop off the four-wheeler and walk over to the tree, wondering what is waiting there for us.

"See that marking up there?" He grabs my hand, pointing about twenty-five feet up the tree, which is surrounded by loads of branches.

"Yeah, what is it?" I squint, straining my eyes to read the scrawled markings.

Can't Beat the Heart of a Carolina Girl

"Well, when Momma and Daddy had been dating for about a month, they came down here one day to go fishing in the pond. When they were packing up their gear, Daddy was being crazy and chased Momma around with a lizard he found. Momma climbed the tree like a spider monkey, and Daddy was so impressed that he followed her up there to sit with her. That's when he carved their names in the tree. I don't believe in good luck charms or anything, but that tree is something special," he explains.

"That's pretty amazing how it worked out like that," I agree, sliding my hand over the rough tree bark.

"Well... do you think maybe... we could?" Carter asks shyly, squeezing my hand. My eyes flit to meet his in pleasant surprise. Our second date, and he's asking me if I think we'll actually fall in love one day. Oddly enough, I already know what my answer will be. From the moment I saw Carter, deep in my heart, I knew there was something special about him. Due to my own stubborn nature, I just overshadowed the miracle God was trying to show me because of Brett.

"Yes," I answer, feeling no sense of denial.

Carter appears shocked, despite my confident reply. "Really? Riley, if you don't want me to, that's okay, too..." Carter flips the knife closed. "I mean, I don't have a lizard anyway," he continues, his adorable awkwardness in full swing.

Delving deeper into his eyes, I study them. In them, I see nothing but love. Now, you may think it's a little too early for me to be falling in love, but I don't know any other word to describe what I feel whenever Carter comes to mind. I take his hand again. "Carter, behind your blue eyes, I can see what we could be," I quote my poem from English, "and I know we haven't been together long at all, but when I first saw you, I don't know… I had this feeling that you'd be around a while. I just didn't know why until now."

Carter fumbles, dropping his knife, and recovers by hugging me tight. "I was hoping you'd say that!" I giggle as he picks up the knife again and makes his way up the tree.

He gets about twelve feet up when he looks down at me. "Just so you know, I'm terrified of heights, so consider yourself adored by me doing this gesture."

Thinking he can't get any cuter, I offer, "Well, where you're at looks like the perfect spot to me."

I can see his laughs form in the chilly twilight air above me. "Gosh, thank you! I'm not as coordinated as Momma, and I think I weigh more than Daddy did when he climbed up there!" Settling onto a sturdy branch, he pulls his knife from his pocket and starts carving. "Riley Houston & Carter Pickett, forever and always," he reads as he finishes, smiling back down at me.

"Forever and always," I repeat, savoring the promise of the words. "I'm so glad that Trent introduced us."

Carter closes his eyes at the memory. "So am I." Skittishly, he maneuvers down the tree before hopping down.

Steadying himself upon his awkward landing, he continues, "He may take advantage of us, but I think we really owe him for this. Well, it's getting dark out; we'd better start heading back to the house." Encompassing me with his arm, he begins to escort me back to the four wheeler.

A chilly wind soon settles into the evening air, causing Carter to pull me in tighter. "So, have you had fun tonight?"

"To be honest, this has been one of the best nights of my life," I admit, meeting his eyes, thick strands of blonde hair blowing in my face.

"Here, let me get that," he whispers, stopping in his tracks as he gently brushes it behind my ear. He allows his hand to linger on my cheek, caressing it softly as he did in my dream. Blushing slightly at the memory, I explore deeper into his eyes, waiting for the moment.

His eyes pore over my face, stopping at my lips. This produces a small smile, yet he allows it to fall as he leans forward. As I watch the pools of blue fade behind closed eyelids, I finally experience the feeling I've been longing for. His lips meet mine, acting as a catalyst that busts the cocoons of the millions of butterflies that have been occupying my stomach for the past few weeks. As they flutter about, my cheeks begin to burn red, as I had not expected to earn this sweet surprise tonight. Our lips separate eight seconds later, and as I open my eyes, I discover Carter staring at me as if I'm his sole focus in this world.

"What is it?" I smile, my words stifled by the intensity of the kiss.

Carter laughs quietly, tilting his head slightly. "You know how often I've prayed for this to happen? To be here in this moment with you? Heck, to just be with you?"

I shake my head, caught up in the fact that he's even admitting this.

"Well, turns out that God's showed me that the outcome's even better than I could've ever imagined on my own. I'm beyond thankful He got us together."

"Amen, Carter," I agree, stepping closer to kiss him again. "Amen."

⌘

Carter and I pull back into the shop at a quarter to eight, parking the ATV and locking the shop before we head back inside. We're about to step into the house when he smiles like a goober, making me laugh. "I'm not trying too hard, am I?"

"Nope. A total sweetheart is absolutely perfect to me," I whisper, giving him a peck on the cheek.

"Ooh... Mommy! Carter got kissed on the cheek!" We turn around to see a little hazel-eyed girl that resembles Carter's mother standing at the doorway.

"Rachel, go watch *SpongeBob* or something!" Carter attempts to hide his frustration as he shoos her away.

Discouraged, she goes back inside, sticking her tongue out at her brother in the process.

Carter makes a face at her as she shuts the door. "That's my little sister. She's seven."

"Aw, she's adorable!"

"Maybe, but she's got a big mouth." Carter laughs at his own expense. "Wanna go inside? It's freezing out here."

"Sure," I agree, following him back into the house.

Not so much to my surprise, Rachel is waiting for us in the living room. "Carter and Riley standing on the porch. He got kissed on the cheek, but wanted one more," she sings, waving her hands like a conductor at each syllable.

Carter chuckles to himself, whispering to me, "Pshh child, you don't even know the half of it!" He winks as we plop down on the couch.

"Lord, have mercy." I can't help but grin at his crazy comment.

Carter studies me, a soft smile playing on his lips. "You're really cute when you laugh." He slides his arm around me, running his fingers over my shoulder.

I turn to him, causing him to raise his eyebrows. "What're you smiling at?"

"You're so sweet." I rest my head on his shoulder. "I don't know why I didn't notice that about you earlier. This is everything I could ever hope for."

The double beeping of a car horn interrupts our conversation. "Must be Momma," I acknowledge, standing up unwillingly.

"Here, I'll walk you to the door." Carter follows, reaching for my hand.

As we stand under the porch light, Carter clears his throat. "Is there any way I can see you again before Christmas?"

Squinting in order to produce a thinking expression, I reply, "I'm sure I can squeeze you in somewhere."

My boyfriend grins, kissing me on the forehead. "Oh yeah?"

"Woo!" Remy snickers out of the window from the back seat of the Pacifica.

I turn to Carter, feeling the need to explain. "Just wait 'til Rachel gets older. It doesn't change!"

119

"No doubt!" Carter laughs, waving at our audience.

"Well, I guess I better get going," I acknowledge, pulling him into a hug.

Resting his head on my shoulder, he whispers, "I'd kiss you goodnight, but I want to get to know your parents before I go making moves like that in front of them."

Stealing another quick kiss on the cheek, I giggle. "I understand. I know they'll adore you, though. I mean, how can they not?"

"Yo, we've got fresh sausage balls and sugar cookies waiting at the house!" Remy pipes in, Momma snapping at her to hush.

"Well, I guess this is goodnight. Remy's acting like she's about to starve." I glare in the direction of the car, unamused.

"Goodnight Riles. Let me know that you got home safe." He smiles, releasing my hand. Carter remains standing on the front porch until he sees that I make it to the car, then waves goodbye.

Momma grins at the look on my face as I open the passenger door. "So, I'm guessing you had a good time tonight?"

"One of the greatest I've ever had." Reminiscing the past few hours, the four wheeler ride, the carving, our first kiss,

Allyson Kennedy

I have already claimed tonight as one of the highlights of my life, all thanks to Carter Pickett.

Chapter Twelve

January 5, 2009 marks my first day back at school for the second semester. My Christmas vacation was amazing, especially after my first real date (with a decent guy that is, as Remy put it), and my first kiss, but we've already discussed all that. Carter and the rest of our friends got together during Christmas break to exchange the gifts we had bought one another. While I gave him a couple of C.S. Lewis novels, he surprised me with a new writing notebook and a set of my favorite pens. "Make some beautiful poetry with this, Riles," he had said, smiling wide as if he, too, knew that he'd made this Christmas the best one I've ever had.

I walk into Linwood Whaley High with a huge smile on my face and proceed to the staircase in the middle of the school, where Lexie and Taylor are waiting. The first day of school, I never thought that five months later I'd have friends, let alone a boyfriend. My life has taken a turn for the better, and I thank God for it all.

"What's up, Mrs. Pickett?!" Taylor laughs as I reach them.

"Hey now, quit that! How did Christmas break go for y'all?" I ask, giggling nonetheless.

"I got a boyfriend!" Lexie smiles, singing each syllable.

122

"Oh my gracious, and you're just now telling me? Who is this gentleman, dare I ask?" I probe incredulously, wondering why she hasn't offered any prior details.

"Devon Turner; he's my neighbor. He asked me to dance at the Black and White Ball while T-squared was plotting your moment with Carter, and it all kinda fell into place after that. Don't have a heart attack, Riles, he just asked me out yesterday! What about you?"

I blush. "Well… I went to Carter's house one night, and… we had our first kiss!"

Lexie high-fives me, which I feel is a rather appropriate reaction, while Taylor replies, "Dang, sounds like y'all had awesome vacations! All that happened to me was I got a new camera for Christmas and Trent prank-called me five times."

I snicker, finding her obliviousness hilarious. "You know, when a boy picks on you all the time, it probably means he likes you."

Taylor is quick to counter my assertion. "Trent likes me? No… no! That will *never* happen. Riley, you're crazy if you think I'd *ever* go out with him!"

"Am I? Y'all even admitted to having crushes on each other when you were little!" I point out. Taylor rolls her eyes, only because she knows the truth behind my claim.

"Oh look, here he comes now." Lexie points, grinning mischievously.

"Do I have anything in my teeth?" Taylor asks anxiously, gritting her teeth at us.

"No, you're good," Lexie and I snicker in unison.

"Howdy Riley, Lexie... Taylor," he finishes, feigning a lack of emotion.

"Hello to you too, Trent Liam Houston," Taylor retorts in the same monotone.

"Dang, when are y'all going to drop the Liam thing? Anyway, I heard about your dates with my buddy, Riles."

I smile smugly. "Yeah, and I heard about your never-ending phone calls with mine."

This makes my cousin blush. "Those were prank calls, Riley. Quit being a smart aleck." He then flips his gym bag over his shoulder and hustles down the hall to catch up with Jesse and Jeremy.

Meanwhile, Taylor is watching him leave, the same love-struck goober smile she mentioned in Earth Science present and accounted for on her face.

"So, you *don't* like him?" Lexie solicits, obviously as amused by this as I am.

"Nope, even though he smelled amazing," Taylor admits.

"He drowned himself in Axe. Half the guys in school smell like that," I point out.

124

"Wow, Trent was right, Riley; you are a smart aleck," she states blandly as the bell for first period rings above us. With that, she stomps off, leaving Lexie and I standing here.

"She's got it so bad." Lexie laughs, shaking her head.

"Yeah, I need to repay them for helping me get with Carter," I muse. The vice principal walks by, shooing everyone to go to their classes. "See you at lunch!" I call as we head to different wings of the school. P.E. is now my first period class, and I'm anything but thrilled about it.

⌘

As soon as I set foot in the gymnasium lobby, I catch sight of Ms. Johnson. Oh, perfect. She's the softball coach, and guess who is on the team since cheerleading season has ended? Hailey Carson and the rest of her skank club. Thinking it can't get any worse, reality kicks me in the butt when they themselves walk in.

Hailey, Tiffany, and Nichole—in that order—all wear matching outfits as if they're trying to channel Barbie or something. Rolling my eyes, I lean back against the brick wall. Why, Lord?

"Like, ohmigosh! Ms. Johnson! Like I had no clue you'd be our gym teacher!" Hailey screams, jumping around like a baboon during feeding time at the zoo.

"Of course she did, her dad paid the guidance counselor just so she'd get her. Why I'm in here too, I have no earthly clue," I think aloud.

"Same here," I hear a voice say from behind me. Pivoting around, I'm faced with a dark-complexioned girl with shoulder-length hair wound in tight curls.

"Hi, I'm Adrienne. I guess you can't stand Hailey either. What's your name?"

"Riley," I answer. "And yeah, we've been on bad terms since the fifth grade."

"How have you survived that? She was in my chorus class last semester and I could hardly bear it!"

"I'm still trying to figure that out." I laugh. "But it's a daily struggle."

Though Hailey and her group are standing on the other side of the room, we can't help but hear them talking over everyone. "Ohmigosh, Nichole! Why didn't you tell me that Chad said that before! I like so totally love him!" Hailey screeches, slapping her friend's arm in excitement.

"Like, ow! Hailey, I just found out this morning while I was talking to him on Facebook chat!" Nichole replies, rubbing the now sore spot.

"Nick, that's no excuse! You could've texted me!" Hailey complains, pulling out her pocket-sized mirror, admiring her complexion. "I'd drop anyone to get that."

126

"Hope she doesn't break the mirror," Adrienne comments, not caring if anyone hears her.

"Yeah, I know. Those eyes could turn someone to stone," I agree, turning to face her again. "And anyway, she's going out with Brett Harvey. I don't know why she would even care about Chad."

Apparently, the Preps somehow overhear us over their own bellowing, because they bust up in our business immediately.

"Riley, it's like none of your business why I was talking about Chad. It's like so totally obvious that he's head over heels for me!" Hailey scowls, flipping her hair out of her face.

"It kind of is my business since I know you're dating Brett," I defend.

"Shug, I thought I, like, told you already, Brettie's mine. So go on back to that Joseph guy in homeroom."

Narrowing my eyes at her, it's all I can do to remain calm. "Listen to me. Brett and I aren't friends anymore, but that doesn't mean that I don't care about him. If you do anything to hurt him, you're going down, too. Do you understand me, or do I have to get your bribed P.E. teacher to come explain it?"

They all stand in silence, including Adrienne. "That's what I thought," I conclude. Hailey rolls her brown eyes with hatred, storming off to the bathroom with her entourage following like ducklings. "Oh, and it's Joel, not Joseph. You can go out with him after you get bored with Chad. I've got Carter Pickett, Shug," I call in a mocking tone as they slam the door.

The whites of Adrienne's eyes stand out drastically from her chestnut skin as she stares, wide-eyed. She smiles, impressed. "Well, Riley, my first impression of you was a soft-spoken kid. I never thought you'd do something like that! That was awesome!"

"Thanks, that's been happening more and more lately," I sigh, still amazed at myself for doing that. Ms. Johnson finally finishes flirting with the boys' baseball coach and proceeds to call the class roll. Adrienne and I walk over to where our class is meeting, and I can't help but think there's going to be a lot of drama to face if I keep revving up like this.

⌘

Second period: World History. By the class description that was emailed to me over Christmas break, it sounds like a snore-fest and a half, but I walk in to find at least three familiar faces: Taylor, Adrienne, and Joel. Being that the latter two are sitting together, I opt to sit next to Taylor.

"Oh Riley, you're in this class? Awesome! We can split the work between us like we did in science!" She laughs, fist bumping me.

"That's what I was planning on doing!" I reply, pulling out my binder.

"So, do you and Carter have any classes together this semester?"

"I wish. He's taking more electives this semester, like shop and agriculture. My sweet country bumpkin," I gush.

Joel butts in, rolling his eyes. "Country bumpkin? You've gotta be kidding me. What's his IQ, like 25?"

Peeved at his comments, I'm quick to correct him. "No, actually he's really smart. Last time he checked, he was sixth in the class. What are you?"

He mumbles, "I don't know, like 37th."

"Why are you asking, anyway?" I question with a hint of curiosity.

"Oh, Joel's just got a huge crush on you," Adrienne blurts, eyeing her friend.

Joel blushes, glaring at her from behind his glasses. "No, I don't."

The four of us immediately fall into an awkward silence, one that for the life of me I yearn to break. "Okay, so who's heard that new song by Daughtry? I think it's awesome!"

129

Thus begins a new conversation until our teacher, Mr. Travers, finally makes an appearance. He passes out a few papers about the class, and as we read over them, I keep catching Joel's gaze flicker in my direction. Realizing he's never acted like this around me before, I feel uneasy, like someone has *told* him I have feelings for him or something. Hopefully, Hailey didn't already start some insane rumor like that about me just for standing up to her, but I wouldn't put it past her.

⌘

As I'm waiting for Momma to pick me up this afternoon, Carter rushes up behind me, exclaiming, "Riley, I can't believe you'd do this to me!"

"What'd I do?" I turn to face him, bewildered.

Taking out his cell phone, he reveals a text message from some random number:

FWD: Riley Houston is so desperate for a guy that she asked Joel Connors out!

"That's such a stupid lie! Carter, I'd never do that. Who'd you get it from?" I interrogate, feeling betrayed.

"Hailey had it forwarded to as many people as she could."

"Ugh, I just want to wring her too-skinny-to-support-a-brain neck! Carter, please don't be mad. Cheating on you is the last thing on my mind," I plead, seeking grace in his eyes.

"It's alright, Riles; I was just picking on you, Sweetheart," he whispers, wrapping his arms around me and kissing my forehead.

"Thank you. I promise that's one thing I'll never do, unlike her wanting to cheat on Brett. Wait, that's it!" I smile ecstatically, the greatest of all ideas sparking in my mind.

"What is it?"

"She starts a rumor after I ticked her off, so now I'm going to tell everyone the truth about her!" I pull out my phone and start a new text message, **"Hailey Carson is cheating on Brett Harvey with Chad Weston!"**

As I'm typing, I can detect the disappointment in Carter's voice. "Riley, you know that when you fight fire with fire everything burns, right?"

Facing him again, I acknowledge my bad judgment. "I guess so," I admit, closing my phone and jamming it back into my pocket.

"That's my girl." Carter smiles, pecking my cheek.

"It's just that she's such a... well, you know," I whine, burying my face in his shoulder.

"Yeah, I know. Just try not to let her bother you. Remember, you're Riley Houston. You're amazing, and you can do anything because God's on your side... even put up with Hailey." He laughs, ruffling my hair.

"Yeah, well, it's kind of hard to do that when everyone's going to believe that lie," I point out, grabbing his hand off my hair and smoothing it back down, laughing nonetheless.

Carter shakes his head, pulling me close. "Don't worry; I'll believe you and stand by you even if no one else will."

I can't help but beam at his comment. "I seriously have to think of a way to thank Trent for finding me the perfect guy."

"Oh, it was nothing," Trent interjects, walking toward us. He pats my shoulder. "Sorry about the whole Joel thing."

"Thanks," I reply, tired. "I just wish she'd leave me alone."

The words leave my lips, and Carter's dad pulls up, offering Trent a ride home as well. And here I am, left standing alone. At least my guy stood with me for the last three minutes before pickup.

Chapter Thirteen

To alleviate my mind of the crazy accusations imposed on me today, I choose to ride the golf cart around the backyard. It may sound a little weird, but this is what I usually do when I need to think something over. It's rather peaceful actually, despite the morbid landscape of the backyard, what with the barren trees, dead grass, and all that. As I'm making a figure eight around a couple of trees, I catch sight of Brett sitting in his backyard. Thinking about what I overheard about Hailey and Chad earlier in P.E., I consider it my duty to go warn him.

"Hey, Brett," I say cautiously as I walk over. It's been at least two months since we last spoke, and I'm kind of regretting the fact that I even came over here as I speak.

His grave eyes do anything but help my confidence. "What?"

Though his tone seems threatening, I proceed. "I need to tell you something about Hailey."

Brett glowers. "If you're just going to tell me that she's a skank and that I should be dating you, then I don't want to hear it."

I narrow my eyes at him, unable to resist a comeback. "Why would I want her leftovers?"

"Riley, if you've come over here to insult me, then go on back home. Hailey's already ruined my day; please don't add to it."

Brett's apparent discomfort sparks my empathy. "What happened?"

He picks up a piece of pine straw, twisting it between his fingers. "Well, you know how much I listen to Jeff Foxworthy the comedian, right?"

"Yeah," I answer, remembering how he used to tell all those jokes to me as we walked to class.

"Well, he's doing a show next month at the events center in Kingston, and Hailey keeps telling me that it's a waste of money. She thinks he's too 'redneck' and says he's a bad influence on me. It's so stupid."

I roll my eyes. "Typical Hailey."

Brett chuckles. "So, what were you gonna tell me?"

"Well, um... you know Chad Weston, right?" I begin warily.

"Yeah, I think so. Ain't he that senior guy all the freshman girls think is 'soooo hot'?" He waves his hands around in a girly fashion for emphasis.

"Yeah. Well, um... I was in P.E. today, and I heard Nichole and Hailey talking, and well..."

"Ugh, I'm sick of that airhead. What did they say?"

134

"Well, Nichole told Hailey that Chad said he likes Hailey on Facebook this morning."

Brett frowns, a gesture depicting that he's now plotting Chad's demise. "And what did Hailey say?"

In actuality, I don't want to tell him, because I don't know how he'll react. Brett's supposed to be a tough and rugged athlete, the rock solid foundation of the Linwood Whaley High football team, but what if he just breaks down under the circumstances? Whatever the outcome is, I can't turn back now.

"She said, 'Ohmigosh! Like why didn't you tell me before, I like totally love him. I'd drop anyone to get that'," I repeat in almost full verbatim. Any other time I would've snickered at my spot-on impression, but even with the perfect opportunity in front of me, I'm not that heartless.

Brett sits for a moment with a blank expression. He stares out into space for several minutes before putting his head down. "Why, Riley?" he finally speaks, his voice shaking terribly. "Why did I ever put myself through this crap?"

Crouching down beside him, I pat his shoulder. "Brett, it wasn't your fault; it was all Hailey. I tried to tell you she was like this."

Brett stares up at me, tears forming in his eyes. "I guess you're just going to tell me to suck it up and move on, that I brought this entire thing on myself, right?"

"No," I mutter softly, "I'm just sorry all of this happened."

Running his hand through his hair, he leans back and sighs. "Thanks. You're a good friend, Riley."

This takes me by surprise. "Thanks; you are, too." I survey his face. His brown eyes are wet and cold; his dark brown hair has tussled wildly from the wind. He appears so pathetic, so vulnerable. The same as I the day he broke my heart. Now, somehow in the twist of fate, the tables have turned, resulting in his heart being ripped out the same way mine had. Talk about love's revenge.

The hands of time seem to come to a standstill as silence lingers between us. Brett seems as if he's searching for an answer to all this insanity life has brought him. I sit here, waiting for him to speak, or leave, or something. Honestly, this whole situation is pretty awkward. Finally, he speaks. "I'm sorry, Riley."

"What?" I raise in disbelief, turning to face him. One more comment catching me off guard, and I'm bound to fall into the crazy cavern with him and Hailey. After all we've been through, he's the first to apologize? Though I've waited a while to hear these words, I'm kind of feeling like a jerk myself.

"I'm sorry. I should've listened to you. I shouldn't have led you on like that. You liked me for me... you cared about me. Hailey only cares about herself."

"Oh," I respond, not knowing what else to say. I never thought he would actually realize that, though I've dreamt about it for entirely too long.

"I don't even deserve your kindness. I've been such a jerk."

I can't stand to let him smother himself in self-hate. If anyone's at fault, right here, right now, it's me. Brett may have had poor judgment, but that doesn't give me the right to sit here and relish in his pain after what just happened.

"Brett, listen. If anyone's a jerk here, it's me. I'm the one who is letting you down yourself for getting your heart broken just for my personal enjoyment," I admit. Dang, I loathe to admit it.

"Oh, I get it. I guess I put you through the same kind of thing that day," he realizes. Instead of offering more, I want to avoid returning to that moment, so I simply nod. He puts his hand on my shoulder. "How about this: let's start over." He holds out his hand for me to shake. "Hi, I'm your neighbor, Brett Harvey."

I laugh, though I'm still skeptical, and shake his hand. "Nice to meet you, Brett. I'm Riley Houston."

His eyes gleam as they investigate mine. "Riley, I'm going to break up with Hailey. There's no reason for me to stay when I'm obviously not wanted."

137

"That's great. I'm proud of you, showing that spray-tanned Prep what she's worth," I encourage, leaning back on my elbows.

He laughs. "Thanks. Now I need to clear things up with someone else."

Baffled, I prod, "What do you mean?"

His eyes dive deeper into mine, in an almost intoxicating manner. "Riley, will you give us a second chance?"

My elbows practically collapse beneath me, my eyes wide. What just happened? The guy I once considered to be my dream guy just asked me to take another chance with him? Never in all the scenarios that ran through my head did I ever think he'd ask me this. Truth be told, I don't want him now. Sure, he's apologized. Sure, he could possibly pass for a male model. So what? He's already broken my heart once, and I've found Carter since then. No matter how bad I may feel about saying no, I have to do it. There's no way I'm breaking up with Carter to chase what God has already revealed is not right for me. Besides, there's no way I'm breaking up with Carter, period.

"Brett, I'm sorry, but no."

His proud look of honor suddenly fizzles out into a puzzled expression. "Why? I thought you liked me."

I study his eyes. "I thought I did, too, but then I gave Carter a chance. He's hilarious, he's sweet. With him, I've

138

never had to prove my worth or stay up late at night wondering if he'll ever return my feelings, because he proves to me every day that he does. Brett, we can still be friends, but Carter's shown me he cares about me in ways no one else ever has."

Brett stares down at his feet. "Oh. Now I really feel like an idiot for not giving you a chance. You're a great girl, Riley. One day I hope to find someone as amazing as you."

Rubbing the back of my neck, I attempt to brush off his compliment. "Thanks, and I know you will. Just keep one thing in mind, Mr. Harvey."

"What's that?"

"It's not all about looks. Find someone who focuses more on the big pictures in life instead of all that superficial mess. It tends to help."

"Thanks," he snickers. Reaching his arms out, he pulls me into a hug. "And yeah, I still want to be friends."

"That's more like it," I reply, already praying that this decision won't come back to bite me in the butt.

Chapter Fourteen

Back at school today, I'm quick to be notified that Hailey has expanded upon her rumor about Joel and me. Now she's telling everyone that Joel and I had our first date at some technology expo in Raleigh. Don't get me wrong, I could actually see Joel bringing a girl somewhere like that, just not me.

In History, Joel reenters stare-down mode. I have to set the record straight. "Joel, we need to talk."

"What about?" he asks, pushing up his glasses.

"I know you've probably heard all of those rumors Hailey's been spreading around, right?"

"Yeah, I think they're pretty inventive actually. Borderline awesome."

He smiles; I cringe. "Yeah, but Joel, you know that they aren't true. I date Carter."

He takes off his glasses to clean them, stalling. "Yeah, I know. But, my popularity's shot up tenfold. Plus, you're pretty cool, Riley."

"Thanks. Strangely, I've been hearing that a lot lately," I mumble, rubbing my temples.

Joel contemplates for a minute. "We can get back at her, though, if you want? I could probably hack her phone."

"No, we can't do that. Carter talked me out of it yesterday. And besides, she's already getting her payback today. I told Brett she was thinking about cheating on him and he broke up with her this morning."

"But we can spread that around, can't we?" He takes my confusion as a reason to explain, "Come on, I need something to work with. I don't want to lose my new group."

"That group of gossip-crazed sophomore girls that has been following you around? They're not true friends, Joel, they're like the high school equivalent of the paparazzi. Adrienne is your best friend. Don't you ever forget that," I prompt.

Adrienne approaches us. "Thanks for telling him that, Riley. He blew me off yesterday! Instead of coming over for our weekly Monday night movie marathon, he goes off to the mall with those girls!"

My stern, disapproving stare causes Joel to search for an excuse. "What? They were hot!" His face turns scarlet red at not being able to come up with a better explanation.

"That's still not a good reason to ditch your best friend, and you know it. Especially one that helped you pass French last semester," I insist.

Joel glances down at his History homework, defeated. "I guess you're right. Adrienne, I'm sorry. If you want, you can come over this afternoon and we'll watch all three *Back to the Future* movies again."

Adrienne takes a moment to think it over, running her fingers through her dark hair. "Alright, I guess I will. Just don't do it again."

Joel grins through his braces. "Awesome."

I'm glad Joel and I were able to work this whole mess out. I'm not about to stand here another day and let the self-proclaimed queen of the freshmen ruin my life. Still, though I've opted to take the high road, I'm apprehensive about the fact that she just might murder me if she ever finds out I was the one who told Brett about her secret.

⌘

Lexie and I are practically starving as we enter the lunchroom this afternoon. We're forced to stand in line for about ten minutes before we even reach the serving counter.

"Pizza, please," Lexie requests in her usual bubbly tone. The lunch lady smiles and drops a leg of crispy fried chicken on her tray. "Well, that was unexpected," she mumbles, walking on to the cash register.

"I'll have chicken too, please," I ask nicely. She plops a fat, greasy piece of pepperoni pizza on mine. "Thanks…" I reply as I go to pay for my own food and head to our table.

"Wanna trade?" I propose, nudging Lexie with my tray.

Lexie nods and we swap trays. "I don't know what her problem is! Yesterday I asked for a biscuit, and she gave me a ham sandwich!" Lexie fumes, taking a bite of pizza.

"Maybe she forgot to put batteries in her hearing aid again," I suggest.

"At least the food's decent today. Last semester I promise you that vegetable soup is what made me sick for a whole week," Lexie gags.

"Oh yeah, I think one of the lunch ladies got a misdemeanor for that."

"No way, for real?"

"Yeah, one of the deacons at church is also a cop, and—"

"Riley Houston!" The front cafeteria doors slam shut, revealing a rather irritated Hailey coming my way, with her two brainless clones behind her.

"What do you want?" I exhale, exasperated by her relentlessness.

"Like, Hailey's here to ruin your social status, you troll!" Tiffany chirps as she pulls out her iPhone to reply to a message.

"Social status? Are you kidding me? So I've made a few friends this year. That doesn't mean I have a 'social status'," I reply.

Hailey steps in front of the group, narrowing her eyes at me. "I know you were the one who told Brett about Chad."

I scoff, though I'm actually a bit terrified on the inside. "Sure, maybe I did. I'll admit to it. It's not like I'm scared of you: the evil pink monster who wears her clothes too tight." Lexie snorts at my comment until Nichole and Tiffany retaliate with the death stare.

Hailey sneers, "Well, well, well. It looks like Ms. Loner has a mouth on her. But, even though you've completely ruined my relationship with that ignorant hick, I still got what I wanted: the hottest senior in school as my boyfriend. Do you want to know why?"

I pretend to care. "Because you're a brat?"

"No. It's because *I* am Hailey Carson. Head cheerleader on the J.V. team, the best pitcher on the softball team, and voted the prettiest girl in the school yearbook eighth-grade year... get the point?"

Remembering the lavish event, I butt in, "Didn't your mom sneak in and stuff the ballot box when we voted for that?"

She peers down at me with a glare that suggests she's going to annihilate me. I don't know what the heck she's going to do. Finally, she bends down just enough to make full eye contact, her demon pupils aglow. "Listen. Riley, you're just a nerd like all of those losers, like Jason and Addison over there. Being a nerd means you have no right to barge into my personal life and force my loving boyfriend to break up with me. Got it?"

I roll my eyes in revulsion. She has to be the most egotistical person I know. It's time to set this she-devil straight. "Hailey, I'm going to tell you one last time. I know that over-applied perfume is intoxicating you, but at least try to understand this. Brett and I are friends. There's nothing you can do to change that. You were willing to hurt my friend just so you could go out with Chad. So the way I see it, you're the real loser here for not actually getting to know Brett for the guy he is. Deep down, he's got a good heart. He may have bad judgment at times—per example, you—but other than that he's okay."

Hailey huffs a breath, smoothing out her denim miniskirt. "I am *not* a loser, Riley Houston. You are, and I will never let you forget that."

The bell rings, and Lexie and I scramble to collect our belongings. Lexie's been silently seething the entire time Hailey's been whining, so she decides to get the last word.

"Hailey, Riley's not the loser here. You aren't either. You're the insane, narcissistic Prep, and I hope you never forget that." With that, she slings her tray into the air. Chocolate milk and greasy pizza remains fly onto Hailey's new outfit that she's been trying to keep pristine all day. Hailey comes to a complete standstill. She and the other Preps have seldom heard Lexie talk, let alone throw food at someone. I snicker, giving Lexie the signal that it's time for us to head back to class. Enough damage has been done for one lunch period.

⌘

The eternal nightmare that is Geometry is the classroom of doom that I enter into for fourth period. I've never been good at math, and now I'm stuck with the teacher who, by Taylor's report, believes that everyone needs to work at a college level in order to earn minimum credit. What does that mean? In common terms, Riley Houston is bound to fail so many quizzes and tests that she's going to feel like a remedial student. Did I mention that this is an Honors class?

Class has been in session for a total of fifteen seconds, and Mr. Park has already had a fit about someone leaving the door open. I may be wrong, but I'm pretty sure that abrupt temper tantrums and unruly high school kids won't mix well. Today he has a new seating arrangement for our class because he couldn't stand the constant talking yesterday. Great.

Ironically, he puts me behind this enormous junior guy who never stops talking. When he begins the lecture, I'm unable to see the whiteboard at all in order to take notes. Every time I stretch my neck to see, the guy moves right back in my line of sight. But hey, maybe now I'll have a plausible excuse to blame my bad grades on in this class.

Mr. Park's explaining about angle measurements when all of a sudden he turns around and smiles. It's the freakiest smile I have ever seen, and it's intended for Adrienne Carr.

"Miss Carr, see me after class," he hisses through gritted teeth. Swiftly, he turns back around to the whiteboard, jotting down another problem. I glance over at Adrienne, who is paralyzed with fear. I wonder what she did; she never gets in trouble, though she's known for her talkative nature. However, based on Taylor's tales from last semester, there's no telling with Mr. Park.

By the end of class, everyone's in a bad mood. He's worked us to the bone with twenty examples on the board. I end up with four pages worth of notes, and we only did one section out of the book. The worst part is that I still don't get the lesson! At least it's Friday and I have the entire weekend to learn it.

Can't Beat the Heart of a Carolina Girl

Everyone exits the class in a raging hurry, except for Adrienne, who waits at Mr. Park's desk. I'm on my way out the door to go home when a few of my lead pencils fall out of my bookbag. As I reach down to pick them up, I can hear Mr. Park yelling at Adrienne.

"Listen, Miss Carr. I know what you were doing during class. Have you no decency than to make that obscene noise?"

Adrienne, practically shaking, glances up at him with big, confused brown eyes.

"You incessantly texted throughout class! The buttons—oh my, the buttons!—clicking away during my lecture! Young lady, this may be your first week in Honors Geometry, but it could also be your last. *Never* do that again, do you understand me?" Mr. Park practically bursts a blood vessel in his forehead.

Considering the fact that Adrienne has yet to blink, I can tell she's beyond freaked out. She nods and flees the classroom, catching me still bent down on the floor, listening. "Nosy much?" she asks, obviously annoyed by the scene.

"Nope, just picking up pencils off the floor," I reply, holding up the purple one. "I couldn't help but hear what he said. That was random."

Adrienne twirls her finger around one of her black curls. "I know right? I didn't know it was a federal offense to text during class. I thought I was being stealthy."

"Well, you've gotta admit, you are kind of a rebel." I laugh.

She considers her Paramore T-shirt, ripped orange skinny jeans, and Converse, smirking at me. "What makes you think that?"

"Hmm… I guess it's a mystery!" I joke. "But seriously, Mr. Park's strict with his own kids, too. Lee and Ara went to elementary school with me, and they're taking college classes now."

"Geez, and I thought my parents were pushing it. Well, I gotta go. See you later, Nosy!"

"Alright, see you!" I reply, not minding the nickname. I sling my bookbag back over my shoulder and head down the stairs, where I'm startled by a ghost from my past.

"Hey." Brett smiles sweetly. Eerily sweet, in fact. Oh crap, what does he want now?

I reach the end of the stairs where he's at but keep my distance. He made that crazy request yesterday afternoon, and even though I said no, he's probably too stubborn to care.

"I was just wondering if you wanted to ride home with me. I mean, you do live next door and all," he proposes, a half-smile cresting upon his lips.

Casting him a skeptical look, I can't help but wonder why he never asked me that when I actually liked him. I have to think of an excuse. Friends or not, I'm not going to risk my

149

relationship with Carter by being seen with Brett, who months ago didn't seem to care if I was alive.

"Well, Momma's probably parked outside waiting for me now, so you know, gotta ride with her," I remark, heading out the door.

"Oh, that's no problem. I already had my mom tell your mom that I'd take care of it, so I guess you have to ride with me," he adds slyly, his brown eyes wide as he watches me pivot to face him, relishing in my surprise.

I wonder if he can tell that I'm on the verge of boiling, or if he's just too stupid to understand that as well. It hasn't even been a solid twenty-four hours since I explained to him that I only have feelings for Carter. I have no doubt that he's just doing this in an attempt to get me to change my mind. Well, for once in his life, Mr. Harvey's not going to get what he wants. There's no way on this planet that I'm going out with him over Carter. Carter and I made that pact, signed and sealed on the tree: forever and always.

"Well then, whatever. But you remember what we talked about, right? We're friends; nothing more."

Brett chuckles and nods, as if he understood that his plan would fall through from the beginning. "Yeah, I know, it's Carter. I'm not too happy about that, but as long as I get to see you, I'm okay."

If there was a trash can nearby, I'd throw up. That's the sickest line of bull I've heard in a while. Just months ago he said he never wanted to be more than friends. I guess Hailey's limited attention span has rubbed off on him.

Unwillingly, I follow him out to the school parking lot to his Chevy, parked near the entrance to the football field. To my surprise, Tiffany is sitting in her convertible, making out with Jeremy. Okay, to tell you the truth, that honestly doesn't surprise me nearly as much as what happens next.

"Sorry, the truck's a mess. I haven't had a chance to clean it out since football ended," Brett apologizes as he turns the key in the ignition switch. At the sound of the truck starting, Tiffany emerges from her daze, pinpointing the newest rumor to turn through her mill. Driving off, I catch sight of her in the side mirror snapping pictures with her phone. My world freezes suddenly; I know exactly what is going on in that sick head of hers. My life is about to turn into a tabloid cheating festival, all because of one stupid former crush.

Chapter Fifteen

We reach the house at a quarter after three, though I feel as if it has taken years. I don't offer conversation during the ride; as soon as Brett parks, I mutter a goodbye and bolt into my house. With the allegations now facing me, spending as little time with him is my best option. My only option.

The walk up the stairs to my room has never felt this elongated before. The fifteen steps seem like a thousand, and by the time I actually reach my room, it feels as if my heart is palpitating out of control from anxiety. Countless thoughts blow through my mind like leaves in a hurricane. What if Carter believes the misleading content of the picture? Shoot, I knew from the moment that photo was taken that he was going to be the first to know. The Preps know where my allegiance lies, yet they can't resist the power of manipulation.

Collapsing on my bed, I hold my stuffed bear, Beary, close. I was three when I named him. Don't laugh—the way I see it, snuggling up to my favorite stuffed animal is a much better coping mechanism than engorging myself with ice cream. Which, by the way, happens to be my second choice.

I lay here an hour and a half, considering the outcomes. Carter is going to hate me, I decide. Just as soon as my life appears to be going somewhere; when I reach the point of contentment. In the midst of all the worst scenarios I can fathom, my phone rings.

Springing up, I cringe when I read the caller ID. The name *Carter Pickett* has never looked so frightening. I'm not going to be the person to screen his call. If he's planning on fussing me out, then let him. None of this is my fault. I know I haven't done anything worth ruining this relationship for. He'll just have to accept the truth. I pray that he will, though by the way the scenario looks, the odds aren't exactly in my favor.

"Hello?" I squeak, my anxiety heightening.

"Hey Riley, it's Carter." He sounds calm; maybe he hasn't heard anything yet.

"Hey. I didn't see you at school today. I missed you." *I miss him*, yeah, that doesn't sound like a lie a cheater would use as a cover up.

"I've missed you, too," he answers, now sounding hesitant. Oh, crap. "Can I ask you something?"

I gulp. He knows. "Sure, anything." The words leave my lips with the utmost caution.

"Someone sent me this picture earlier..." he starts, sounding unsure of himself. "You and Brett and just friends, right?"

Cold tears leak down my cheek, causing me to shiver. No matter how blue my eyes may be, they feel black to the core. Carter saw the fabrication, and our relationship is done for.

"Yes, Carter. Brett and I are just friends. Despite what anyone is trying to tell you, I don't have feelings for him anymore. I know Tiffany sent you a picture this afternoon; I saw her take it. Please, please believe me. The last thing I want is to lose you."

Forget the few tears, my vision grows blurry as the silence prolongs between us. How is he supposed to believe me over a piece of concrete evidence? If we were in court right now, I would be convicted, no doubt about it.

After what seems like an eternity, he puts my nerves at ease. "Riles, don't talk like that. Of course I believe you."

"Really?" my voice trembles, my throat constricting and burning as I try not to cry over the phone.

"Of course! You've never been anything but honest with me. Why should I believe them over you?" Carter admits, his voice anything but angry.

How can he be so sweet? If I had ended up anywhere else in the world, there would be no one, no one that would ever treat me the way that he has. At this very moment, I can at last put a name to the overwhelming adoration I have for him. Somehow, despite my former resistance, I've fallen in love with Carter Pickett. How it has happened in a month and a half mystifies me, but could God be trying to tell me something through this? Apparently, Carter—being a heck of

154

a lot smarter than me—pinpointed it long ago. Meanwhile, I was preoccupied trying to make my own plans work, and look where that mess has gotten me. My top priority now is to make up for every second I've dismissed his affection, starting with admitting this newfound information.

"Carter, let me make this all up to you. Can you come over for supper? Momma's making fried chicken and cornbread." My voice clears up instantaneously. It's amazing how this boy can change my attitude in a heartbeat.

"Yeah, Dad can drive me over. See you in a little bit, Shug," he agrees. I can almost hear him smiling through the phone. We say our goodbyes and I close my phone, though I'm dying to hang on to the sound of his voice. Corley Creek feels as if it's five thousand miles away from Grahamwood tonight.

⌘

I grin from ear to ear as I peer out the front door's side glass at the sight of a white Ford truck pulling into the driveway. Carter says bye to his daddy, trudging through the frozen grass and climbing the brick steps of the porch. I don't allow him a chance to ring the doorbell before I open the door for him.

Can't Beat the Heart of a Carolina Girl

Carter smiles, waltzing in. "Someone's eager to see me!"

"Come on in, you crazy thing!" I reply. We both settle on the couch, and as we do, my entire body feels as if it's entering paralysis. Whenever I catch sight of him looking at me, all I can think about is the fact that I am about to open my heart to someone for the first time. A haunting doubt unsettles me further, contemplating if he even loves me back. And of course, trepidation ensues.

Carter grabs my hand, interlocking our fingers. I pray he won't notice the instant transformation the tint of my face is taking, but he turns to face me.

"What's wrong Riles? I don't think I've ever seen you this anxious." Concern envelops his voice as he holds my hand in his, tracing my knuckles.

"Sorry, I'm still a little worried about that picture Tiffany sent out. Brett's been relentless, and I'm almost regretting our agreement to be friends. I don't know why he can't grasp the fact that you're the only one I'm interested in." My eyes sting from holding back a resurfacing round of tears.

Carter reaches over, his kiss grazing my cheek. "I know, I know. Just try to ignore them and all the crap they're putting you through. It's not worth it to give them exactly what they want: you being tortured." He brushes my side-bangs from my eyes, making the memory of our first kiss resurface.

He's being so sweet; if anything, he deserves to be told now. I lay my head on his shoulder and whisper, "Carter, I—"

"Riley, Carter! It's time to eat!" Remy yells, barging into the living room. Darn it, I've lost the chance to a ten-year-old. At least the fried chicken will make up for it.

Remy locks her eyes on Carter and exhibits a toothy, yet mischievous grin. "Dang Riley, he looks too good to be your boyfriend!" As if I need another confidence decimator right now.

"Remy, don't you have some chicken to go drool over?" I remind through gritted teeth, blood pressure spiking.

Remy shakes her head, oblivious to my agitation. "In a second." She skips over to the couch, plopping down next to Carter. I roll my eyes, though I can't help but snicker at his expense.

"You must be Remy..." Carter proceeds with caution, remembering our previous conversations about her.

Remy flips her dark brown hair off her shoulder in a way eerily similar to Hailey (which gives me the creeps, for the record). "Why, yes I am. You must be my future husband because you don't know how many of my dreams you've been in!"

Carter's blue eyes bulge at me in bewilderment, and I can't help but start laughing. "Sorry Remy, but I'm completely taken by your sister, and she's beautiful. You're lucky to have a sister as sweet and humble as her," he explains, shifting his gaze to meet mine.

My heart goes into overdrive at his words, though it's obvious Remy's a bit perturbed at his answer. "Well, you can't blame me for trying. If anyone's lucky here, it's Riley. You're a great guy."

I revisit Carter's eyes, which are glowing. He's the *greatest* guy, and tonight I'm determined to let him know... after supper.

At the dining room table, Momma and Daddy jump all over Carter with questions. Who are you kin to? What year did your daddy graduate from high school? Where does your momma work? It's so embarrassing, but at least they seem to like him. Between bites of chicken I try to say something, anything to change the subject, but I can't get a word in. Hopefully, Carter doesn't mind, though I can tell he's nervous.

"So Carter, how did you and Riley meet?" Daddy asks.

Carter smiles over at me, excited to be able to tell our story. "I'm a friend of Trent's. He introduced us in science last semester. I guess we had chemistry!" I can tell his joke was inspired by nerves, so I laugh to make him feel less awkward. He just makes the whole thing so cute.

"Oh, I remember Riley telling Remy and me about that after the Black and White Ball. She seems to like you a lot," Momma reminisces. Everyone turns their attention to me, and I start blushing again.

Carter saves me. "Yeah, she's an amazing girl. I'm so glad I've gotten to know her."

His hand slides into mine underneath the table, and I kick his foot playfully. "I'm glad we met, too. You're one of the best things to ever happen to me."

Remy gags to herself, Momma giving her a nudge to be polite. As everyone finishes up, I invite Carter to go outside. A moonlit Carolina night is always romantic, and I have a deed to do. We settle onto the steps of the back porch, freezing, as January is always the cruelest of the winter months. I sit shivering, gripping his hand. I'm so stupidly nervous that I forgot to grab my coat.

Noticing this, he takes off his Carhartt coat. "Here, take this. I don't want you to freeze to death."

"Thanks, but I can go back in the house and get one out of the closet." I attempt to stand up. "There's no need for you to freeze on my behalf."

He pulls my face closer to his, so close that his eyelashes tickle my cheek. "But then you would have to leave. This way I can do this." His tender kiss elicits shockwaves, his hand caressing the side of my face. God's constructing the perfect moment.

"Carter, I've never met anyone like you," I begin once our lips part, the words flowing out of me before I even know which direction to take.

Thankfully, he takes my pause as an opportunity to speak. "Why do you say that, Riles?"

I grip his hand tighter, snuggling closer into his shoulder. "I've never met anyone who's given me a chance like you have. No one has ever been a confidant to me before, no one has ever given me the benefit of the doubt when all the evidence is stacked against me. No one's ever made a promise to stand by me like you have, and Carter, that means more to me than you'll ever know."

Carter's at a loss for words, scaring me stiff, but after a moment he replies, "Thank you for allowing me to be all those things for you, Riley. I wouldn't be able to do it if I didn't have something to stand for, and I hope you know that promise still stands. I never plan on sitting down for you, either. If we're together, I'm going to do everything in my power to work at our relationship, because in my world, the thought of us ending brings me the most pain."

Watching him express his dedication to our relationship, I'm confident these words were destined for him since the moment God placed me on this earth. No words have ever left my lips so easily. "Carter, I love you."

He blinks fast, a tear emerging from the pool of blue in his eyes, and smiles that famous goober smile of his. "I love you too, Riles, and I never plan on stopping." Happy tears of my own form, and I wrap my arms around him in an embrace. He kisses me, and it burns, not with rage like I had expected earlier in the day, but with passion.

Allyson Kennedy

As his sweet lips pull away from mine, I whisper, "I pray that nothing will ever come between us, nothing will harm us, and nothing will stop us."

Carter laughs softly, kissing my hand. "Nothing will ruin God's plans."

Chapter Sixteen

The following weeks seem to drag on like a trip through the Sahara Desert with no water. Hailey continues to gossip about how I'm desperately chasing Brett, how I told him about Chad just to break them up—the stupidest lies. I may have had the misconception that he was The One long, long ago, but Carter Pickett will always be beside me every step of the way, and I have his word on that.

By mid-March, I've concluded that Geometry will be the death of me. I have a C-average in there, my lowest class average to date. I'm an Honors student; this isn't like me. Once my parents found out, joy became fleeting.

"Carter can't come over until your grades come up!" Daddy concurs as he stomps downstairs, inaccurate in that he pinpointed my falling average to my new romance. I'm sitting here crying in my room, hating that my parents never seem to understand where I'm coming from. It's not like Carter's to blame for my terrible math skills! Mr. Park seems to hate us all, except for the juniors, because they do so well in there. And for that, I envy them.

As I let out my frustration, my phone rings. Thinking back on the past few months, it seems that it does every time I'm upset. At least it's Lexie and I can vent to her.

"Hey, Riley! I've got an awesome idea, but I wanted to run it by you first," she squeals as soon as I accept her call. Okay, probably not the best time to talk about my problems.

"Sure, go ahead," I answer. My tone doesn't show it, but I'm interested. She hardly ever gets this excited about an idea.

"Well, I've been thinking. You and Carter are always saying how you need to repay Trent for getting you two together, and I think I've finally found the solution!"

"What is it?" I prompt.

"Well, he's single. We could set him up with someone... if you know what I mean?"

I rack my brain for a second, coming up with a rather interesting conclusion. Wait... it can't be. "*You* wanna go out with Trent?"

"Ew, *no*! Devon might have broken up with me last week, but Trent... gosh Riley, how could you say that?" Lexie gags.

I laugh. "Sorry, but I thought that's what you were going to say! Who do you know that'll actually want to go out with him?"

"Well, she's one of our good friends, Riles. I thought it'd be kind of obvious."

Oh... that's when it hits me. "Taylor! Lex, you're a genius! But how are we going to get them together? They act like they hate each other."

"Well, that's why I called you..."

"Okay, thanks bud... wait! I think I actually have a pretty good idea. On Sunday, I'll tell Trent to come with me and my family to eat at McKiver's after church because we need to get together to work on our Home Economics project that may or may not be real. You get Taylor there somehow, and the magic will happen. Carter and I both swear by McKiver's. Trust me, this will work. It'll have to. Taylor's been driving me crazy pretending to despise him."

"Okay, that sounds like an awesome plan! What time do you want us to meet y'all there?"

"About twelve-thirty." I can still hear Daddy grumbling from downstairs, so I take the opportunity to cut our conversation short. "Hey Lex, I hate to let you go, but I still need to study for Geometry. We have a huge test in there tomorrow, and my parents already banned all access to Carter for the time being," I explain, hoping this will be a valid explanation.

"Oh gosh, I'm so sorry to hear about that. Good luck studying for that test! See you on Sunday!" she offers, hanging up.

Well, I didn't get to vent as much as I had wanted to, but at least Trent and Taylor will benefit from this. Unless they attempt to choke us for conspiring the whole thing, that is. Now, it's time to study. Whoopee.

I pull my Geometry binder out of my bookbag and turn to the chapter eight notes. We have been learning about the area and volume of three-dimensional figures for two solid weeks. Mr. Park has used up four of his whiteboard markers in three days. He's mad, we're all terrified, and still only those genius juniors know what he is talking about. I'm sure to make less than a C.

Skimming over the notes, I become more frightened with each passing section. This happens to be our last test before report cards. If I fail it, my grade average will decrease further, and I still won't be able to see Carter. I have to force myself to focus, or else this could be my first and last relationship.

"Okay, for a cylinder, the volume is $V=\prod r^2$, and the area is $A=2\prod r^2+2\prod rh$. This is so stupid! How's one part of the area two times the volume? I'll never pass this test. I might as well join the convent and give up on guys. I'll never be able to see Carter again," I mumble, stabbing my pencil into my notebook.

"Aw, don't hurt the poor notebook, Riley!" I hear a voice outside my door.

"Who's there?" I ask in a precarious manner. I don't recognize the voice automatically, but Brett pops his head through the cracked doorway. Great, this is just what I need, another thing to worry about.

"What are *you* here for?" I ask, uninterested.

"Your dad called and asked if I could help you with Geometry," he replies, taking off his jacket and slinging it over my bedpost. "You okay with that?"

No way—he didn't just do that. He's not home, and I don't want him to feel like he is. But, I'm desperate for help. "Yeah, I guess so. I have no idea what I'm doing." I sigh, brushing off the eraser shavings that cover my notes.

Taking a seat in my desk chair, he rolls over to where I'm at, glancing at my notes. "So, what exactly do you need help with?"

I flip through a couple pages. "Well, I don't understand how I'm supposed to remember the area and volume formulas for all of these figures! I mean, the area of a cylinder is two times the volume plus $2\prod rh$? How am I supposed to remember that in the stress of a test along with all the other ones? Especially with Mr. Park breathing down the back of our necks going 'Hurry up! Hurry up!' It's so—"

Brett takes his hand and covers my mouth, ending my rant. I laugh, despite my current dislike of him. "Thanks for not letting me explode."

"Anytime." He smiles, adding, "And by the way, you forgot the *h* variable for height in the volume formula. That's why it's not making sense. We just need to find ways to help you remember all the variables, and you'll be fine."

Peering back down at my notes, my eye catches the formulas for a sphere. "Okay, how about these?" I point at the examples.

"Okay, so instead of the volume being $A=4\prod r^2$ like the area, add threes to it. The volume is $V=4/3\prod r^3$. See, they're not that different."

"Oh, I think I get it now. That's so much easier than how Mr. Park explained it."

"How *did* he explain it?" he asks, eyes lit with curiosity.

"'Learn these stinking formulas the right way, or you'll fail the class! Why did I agree to teach freshmen?'" I yell in mock anger, waving my hands around savagely and pretending to hurl a pencil at him.

Brett snorts, shaking his head. "Ah, I see he hasn't changed much from when I had his class."

My little tutor session continues on like this until about six-thirty, suppertime. Brett leaves after we discover ways for me to remember all the formulas, declining Momma's invitation to eat with us. To be honest, I'm happy for the break, especially after what happened the other day. But, thanks to him, I actually think I can pass the test now. As much as it annoys me to say it, he can be an okay guy at times.

Can't Beat the Heart of a Carolina Girl

⌘

Walking into Mr. Park's class with a weak smile, I try to put my best foot forward and have a positive outlook on things, yet I can feel the pangs of nervous energy fluttering around in my stomach. I sit in my fifth row seat and get out a pencil, along with a piece of scrap paper. As everyone else files into the room, I'm relieved to see that they also seem uneasy.

Mr. Park runs into the classroom a millisecond before the tardy bell rings, slamming the door behind him. "Algebra 2 just failed their quizzes last period!" He glares in my direction, veins visible on his neck. "You better not let me down." I cringe at the thought. I have to remember what Brett taught me.

Our teacher passes out the tests, delivering one to each desk. "You must do these carefully. Think before you write down your final answers! I'm talking to *you*, freshmen!" He sneers, eyeing Adrienne. I still don't know why he dislikes her so much.

With a tight grip on my pencil, I take a cautious glimpse at the first question. *Find the area and volume of a sphere with the following measurements.* Perfect, this is one of the first examples Brett taught me.

I finish the test earlier than I expect. Mr. Park fires a hostile look my way as I turn in my test. "You had better made higher than a C, Riley." I back away and return to my desk, deciding on the way that I will never become a math teacher. Too stressful.

About twenty-five minutes later, the bell rings and everyone that has finished packs up their things and—let's be honest here—escapes. I decide to go find Carter and ask him how his day's been.

Making my way down the hall, I spot a group of sophomores clustered around a poster on the wall. As I pass by them, I hear laughing and snickering. Turning back around to see what's so amusing, I catch them gaping at me before they retreat down the hall. The poster crashes to the ground face up. Reaching down to pick it up, the horrifying words hit me like a death sentence: *Riley Houston's poem to Brett Harvey.*

My hands tremble as I take in the wrinkled, tattered, tear-stained paper I had thrown in the bushes a few months ago, the day I vowed to shake the grip Brett had on my heart. Now the ghost of my past is haunting me yet again, taped onto a hot-pink poster for the world to see. I know who committed this atrocity almost instantly, as well as the consequences that will be rendered. I'm merely a puppet on a string mastered by the ruler of the insane, Queen Carson.

Quiet footsteps approach from behind me. I do not turn, since I'm in no way ready to step out onto the destructive ledge that lies ahead. Finally, I hear the chilling words. "Riley… can we talk?"

Can't Beat the Heart of a Carolina Girl

My eyelids drift closed as I turn around hesitantly to see Carter, the one I love, greeting me with a solemn disposition. I take a stifled breath. "Yes, Carter," I say, feeling more shamed and insecure by the second.

He takes in the poster for an extended second, then shifts his focus back to me. His face grows grimmer, his eyes duller, and his heart darker. "The poster," he says, his voice quivering. "Riley, I thought 'Blue Eyes' was ours. You wrote it for Brett?"

My eyes trace the ground in complete humiliation. Soft tears form, despite my effort to control them. "Yes, I wrote it about Brett. But that was before…"

"Before what, Riley?" Carter fumes, taking me aback. "Before or after you used me to get him jealous?"

"Used you?" I ask, bewildered. "Carter, I love you. Why would you think that?"

He rolls his eyes, pacing the floor in front of him. "Oh, I don't know. Just that you've ridden home with Brett, you study with Brett, and you always talk about how you used to like him so much. Let's also not forget that he's infatuated with you now." As he pauses, I search for his old semblance in his eyes. What happened to the Carter who never questioned my honesty?

"Carter, you're the only guy I care about. Brett… I don't even know what's going on between him and me, but it's nothing like what you and I have. I did want to be more than friends a while back, but that was before I got to know you." I brush my hands through my hair to keep it out of my face. "Don't you know how much you mean to me? It took every ounce of courage in me to tell you I love you that night. I wouldn't say that to just anyone, especially Brett, after all that's happened."

"You love me. You really love me?" Carter counters with a sarcastic bite. "Riley, if you 'love' me, then why do we keep coming back to this? Why do I keep having to ask myself if you're committed to us?"

I reminisce the last few months of our relationship. I admit, we have had many stressful days, but that doesn't mean I have feelings for Brett. Sure, Hailey's been a pain in our necks, but I thought Carter knew me better than to trust her words over mine. Maybe we don't know each other as well as we thought.

"Carter, I'm… I'm so sorry," is all I can manage, my breathing giving way to worry. His eyes narrow, diverting as I speak again. "I'm sorry I let all this happen. I'm sorry I let Brett take up such a large portion of my life. I'm sorry Hailey's created this wedge between us. But what I'm really sorry about is that if you don't trust me this time, both of us will regret it."

Tears descend down my cheeks as I glimpse at him for an answer. Silence echoes throughout the barren hallway as Carter stares daggers at the ground, caught up in critical thought. Taking the poster from my hand, he soaks in the words written in smudged ink. As his blue eyes skim over the

171

tattered paper, my thoughts skim over the possibilities. Finally, in the midst of it all, he speaks.

"I regret it now." He loosens his grip, allowing the poster to slide from his grasp onto the grimy, dirt-filled hallway floor. Tears stream from my eyes as I hear the patter of his footsteps fade off down the stairway.

Like my first day on campus, I now stand alone. The promise Carter made to me that January night is now decimated. This isn't the Riley Houston that entered Linwood Whaley High School back in August. This is far from what I had hoped my transformation would be like. Hailey Carson has exceeded her quota this time, and I'm not about to let her get her glory from ruining everything I hold close, everything I love, Carter.

Chapter Seventeen

Friday nights are supposed to be adventurous, memorable, or at least a little fun. Yet after an occurrence such as the one this afternoon, all hope of that is depleted. Here I lie—well, mope—on my bed, listening to "Lord Knows" on my iPod and pleading to God for Carter to reconsider and forgive me.

I'm pathetic, I know. You may be thinking, "Big deal, move on! Find another guy!" Any apathetic person out there would, but guess what? Another guy is the last thing my heart desires. Carter and I met for a reason, and I know that being torn apart by a vicious high school cat-and-mouse escapade isn't supposed to be our end-all. We have a connection, a purposeful connection, and my past wishes for Brett Harvey are not going to ruin this for me yet again. My enemies have gone too far this time, but how am I to live with the havoc they've wreaked?

And yet, I have a vastly more important matter on my hands. There's no telling how Carter's feeling. In a bout of selfishness, I pray that he's as miserable as I am: lonely and heartbroken. Never have I felt so downtrodden, knowing he's convinced that my love for him was composed of lies. However, the real lie amid us is what he believes now, that I've never loved him at all.

173

Can't Beat the Heart of a Carolina Girl

As "Lord Knows" ends, I close my eyes, allowing my depleted energy to take over and halt my thoughts. My emotional pain is unbearable. Maybe a little nap will ease my mind.

⌘

A slight tapping sound wakes me up a couple hours later. At first, I assume it's my imagination, so I settle back down to sleep. Over the course of the next few minutes the noise becomes more persistent, so I force myself up and see where it is coming from.

As I walk around my room listening, it sounds like the tapping is coming from my window. I figure it's a deranged bird trying to fly through the window, so I pull back my curtains to check. To my surprise, there's no bird. The only thing I see is a brown-haired boy gazing up at me, throwing pebble after pebble at the glass pane.

"Thank God!" I smile for the first time since school dismissed. I unlatch the window, ecstatic to see him again. "I love you! I'm so sorry!" I scream down, hoping he's here to forgive me.

"Wow, Riley, I thought you hated me!" I hear as my reply. That's not Carter's voice. Wiping away my still sleepy eyes, Brett is soon revealed to be the one standing outside. Can this day plummet any further down the crap hole?

"Brett?! Why are you here? I thought you were Carter," I say, rubbing my temples.

Brett's sudden smile drops as he answers, "To apologize."

My skepticism makes a reappearance. "Seriously?"

He nods. "I'm sorry. Everything that has happened to you this year is my fault. Hailey's drama and every one of your conflicts with Carter... Riley, I never wanted this to happen."

I know I've had my reasons in the past to not believe a word that comes out of the mouth of Brett Harvey, but for once my conscience is leading me to count on him. Would he assist with Hailey's attempt to ruin my relationship with Carter? Never. Deep down, there are more layers to Brett than the selfish womanizer I've accused him of being. In all honesty, he's still somewhat of a good guy. A guy that I have wronged myself.

"Brett, I forgive you. But honestly, I'm sorry for what I've put you through, too."

Brett peers up at me in confusion. "What did you do to me?"

I exhale, blowing my bangs out of my face. "Well, for starters, the Riley Houston we knew wouldn't talk crap to Hailey just because she didn't want you going out with her."

Brett smiles smugly to himself. "What else?"

It's all I can do to not roll my eyes at him. "And the real Riley would have never been such a jerk to you because you didn't like me back, even if you did lead me on. I'm sorry for every hateful thing I've said to you and about you to others. I didn't mean a word of it. I was... jealous."

"Jealous? Why would you be jealous? Especially of someone like Hailey," Brett questions.

"Well, I had wanted to be with you for the longest time. Like, practically since I knew what a crush was. And when I finally thought you felt the same way, she happened," I confess. I'm sure that now he'll think I'm a stalkerish freak.

Brett stands in silence for a second, but relief washes over me when he asks me to meet him outside. Making the walk to the backyard, it feels like this relationship is finally mending after seven months of hate and despair. At last, Brett and I have reached common ground, unless he's about to start another conflict once I arrive.

The sunset peers over the treetops, creating a caramel color that's impossible to ignore. Such a warm backdrop for the coldness I'm feeling inside. Brett smiles as I shut the screen door to the house and sit beside him on the porch step.

Brett reaches into his pocket, pulling out a folded up piece of notebook paper. A quick toss, and it lands on the ground in front of me. I gaze upon the mysterious file, looking back to him for direction. "It's how I really feel," he says with shy hesitation. Picking up the paper without haste, I read the contents:

Walking through the hall

On my way home

I find a tattered paper, displayed for all.

Something's on it, as I pick it up to read

It must have been the poem

You wrote about me.

The tattered paper has tear stains and tears

It must have been one you wrote when you cared.

I fold up my thoughts and continue my walk through the hall

You had feelings for me I never knew of at all

Now I hear you calling me a jerk to your friends

Silently wishing all this torture would end.

Surely, if I offered an apology, both hearts would mend.

But seeing this tattered paper will forever remind me

That loving you will have to remain behind me.

This tattered paper has shown me what I'm worth.

I'm sorry to show you that I'm merely a jerk.

Can't Beat the Heart of a Carolina Girl

Would it be too much to ask,

For you to accept me back?

Please forgive me, sooner or later.

Or will you throw me away again, like this tattered paper?

"I know it's not great," he says as I finish reading, "but it's exactly how I feel. Everything about it's true."

"Wow, I don't know what to say. Brett, it's not bad at all," I confess, though wary. "You really feel this way?"

He speaks softer, leaning in closer to my face, as if we're forced to meet in secret. "Yes, even the line where I wrote, 'loving you will have to remain behind me'. Riley, I think I'm in love with you."

My world ceases to turn at this moment, frozen in time as Brett admits the words I've longed to hear for years—words that are now meaningless. I'm lost in the brink of insanity, screaming out for anyone to save me. But is there anyone? I'm alone with Brett, the same Brett that swore we were just friends months ago, the same Brett that said that's all we'd ever be. But is he really the same? Is anyone I know the same? Lexie's questioning her love life when she's hardly ever cared in the first place. Carter, who once praised me for my honesty, borderline despises me over a lie. And now Brett? Even I'm not myself anymore.

Allyson Kennedy

"I love you, Riley," Brett whispers again. I emerge from my epiphany, silent and solemn. Brett's brown eyes seem to lose their shine as I do not return an answer. For me, for anything. I have no answer.

Chapter Eighteen

Brett left me on the porch tonight after I couldn't fathom up a response to his untimely admission. I've been thinking about the situation for hours. His admittance has placed me in a pure state of shock. How could he love me?

It's been four months in the making that Carter and I have been together. It would be an utter shame to let those days fall into the dark peril of the past. Brett's not making me feel any better by pronouncing his "love" either. There's no way he loves me. Maybe he feels the slightest sense of pity. No sparks fly when he's in my presence. No feelings illuminate my darkened heart. In fact, I'm almost empty inside. All I can admit to now is friendship, all I'll ever be capable of doing.

There are few words to describe how lost I feel tonight, yet I vaguely remember staring up into the stars. Gazing among them, I hold on tight to the warm feeling that overcame us that January night as we sat in this exact spot. The stars shone brighter that night than I'd ever witnessed before, making me wish even more that Carter was back by my side.

My memory fades away at that moment, as I fall asleep amidst my pondering. Dream after insane dream comes to mind, all about Carter coming back to me, holding me, loving me. It seems like a nightmare, more so because it's now only a distant fantasy.

A cold shiver travels along my neck, causing me to wake abruptly to find myself lying in Carter's arms. Somehow I made my way to the bench before I had fallen asleep, basking in the Carolina moonlight. Malicious dream or not, I like this one. It all seems too real.

"Carter, is that you?" I ask drowsily, managing to pick myself up.

The boy looks down on me with the most charming of smiles. "Hey, Riles." His soft voice saying my name makes my heart skip a beat in that familiar way. His calm, chivalrous persona inflicts the most amazing feeling in my wounded heart. This cannot be happening.

"Seriously Carter, is that you?" my tone is stern, praying it's not Brett in disguise again. The fair prince leans over, brushing a strand of hair behind my ear. The gentleness of his touch strikes me as true. There is no doubt in my mind at this moment: Carter Pickett is by my side.

"Riley, I'm sorry I showed up so late, but something made me realize that if I give up on you, I'll be giving up on everything and anything I care about. I'd die inside knowing that I could only love you like a passerby, because that's a world of torture I never want to relive." His beautiful blue eyes form tears as those last few words leave his lips.

I guide my fingers across his face, wiping his forgiving tears away. Crying is usually considered a sign of weakness in a man, yet in this case, Carter comes across as a true man. He's able to admit his feelings, his wrongs, and his desired destiny.

"Carter, it's fine. The truth is, this whole disaster is my fault. 'Blue Eyes', I never should have brought it up as ours. I should have told you from the beginning that I had written it while my heart was blinded by false pretenses. I was completely stupid to even refer back to that. You're the only guy I've ever felt that way about!" My shoulders heave at the mention. His beautiful eyes shine with the greatest intensity. As he pulls me closer, we cry together in the night, the only light available being the stars above.

"Carter, if you want me to, I can tell Brett that I never want to speak to him again. If I had never met him in the first place, none of this would have happened. We would have never had to deal with all of this stupid drama that one crush has caused us. Our lives would be so much better for it."

Carter's smile is full of sympathy as he refutes, "Riles, if you would have never met Brett, then I wouldn't have had the chance to talk to you. Remember that day last November when you found out he liked Hailey?" I nod, still wiping away tears. "If Brett had never led you on, you wouldn't have been heartbroken that lunch hour. That's the first time I ever felt confident that you needed me. I mean, we had talked before and all, but I knew deep down that you didn't feel the same way. That one day, though, it changed my life completely. I swear if it wasn't for God guiding this entire situation in the good, the bad, and the ugly, I would have never had the chance to love the girl of my dreams."

At last, a smile forms behind my tears. He grasps my hand and I soon realize that he's right. About everything.

"And, if Brett was still not a part of your life now, then I would have never realized what a jerk I was not to believe you at school this afternoon."

My curiosity arises. "What do you mean?"

Carter smiles, obviously amused by something I'm unaware of. "Brett called me and told me how much of an idiot I was for leaving you. He said if he couldn't have a girl as amazing as you are, then he was bound and determined to keep you with a guy that deserves your love. I mean, do you really think Dad would've driven me out here this late? Brett came and picked me up."

"Wow, that was sweet of him," I say, astonished.

The boy I love nods, running his thumb over mine. "I'm so glad he did. You're amazing, Riley."

I blush, ready to refute. "I don't understand why you think that. I'm just me, nothing special at all."

Carter stares at me in disbelief. "Because you're modest. Do you think Hailey Carson or Nichole Rogers would call themselves 'nothing special'?" He brings my hand up to his mouth, kissing it softly. "You're incredible, Riley Houston. Don't you ever forget that."

My lips form a weak smile as I pull Carter into a hug. "I love you, Riley," he whispers.

"I love you too, Carter." Within seconds, our lips meet and sparks soar again, a feeling that I had convinced myself I'd never feel again. For the first time in a while, I thank God for Brett Harvey, the "skank-loving pretty boy" whom I swore his only purpose in life was to ruin everything I loved. It looks like there is more to this quarterback than meets the eye. Underneath is a mature, caring individual who I am now honored to call my friend.

Chapter Nineteen

"For the last time, you were asleep when Mrs. Wilson mentioned the project! I volunteered for us to partner up, she noticed you were out cold, all the other girls in the class laughed. Trust me, it was pretty funny," I lie, explaining to Trent for the third time about the fabricated project in our Home Economics class. My family has just arrived at McKiver's Café, our usual eatery of choice after church on Sundays. After the dramatic event Friday night, I'm glad to be able to focus on helping someone else out with their romance problems.

"But I stayed awake in there pretty much every day last week..." he grumbles, attempting to get out of doing work.

"Hey, now," I interject in a piqued manner for effect. "You may have gotten Carter and me together, but that doesn't mean I'm going to do all the work for you, Cuz."

"Alright, alright. But don't expect me to contribute anything meaningful. I don't get that class."

"All that matters is that you help slap some glue on our decorations for the poster," I continue, the door to the restaurant clinking behind us as we enter.

Can't Beat the Heart of a Carolina Girl

"How many?" Lola asks from the seating podium at the entranceway.

"Five," Momma answers, doing a quick head count. Lola then escorts us to a large table, but not before I catch sight of my target. Taylor's wearing a purple, knee-length sundress with a pair of dark brown sandals. Perfect, she looks best in purple, and Trent's already gazing at her.

"Oh Lexie, Taylor! I didn't know you guys would be here!" I say, I'll admit, obvious as all get out. I even go so far as to wink at Lexie, who practically snorts Mountain Dew out her nose.

Shifting my eyes back to Trent, I can almost see the gears turning in his mind. After a moment, he blurts, "What the heck is going on here?"

"An intervention of sorts." Lexie takes the lead, gesturing from Trent to Taylor. "Welcome to your blind date, courtesy of Riley and Carter, with a little help from me."

"Carter would've been here if he'd been allowed..." I mutter, still fuming about the Geometry lecture. Though Carter came over Friday night under special circumstances (he snuck over from Brett's house, to which my parents are still unaware), I'm still under boyfriend lockdown until Mr. Park returns our test grades.

After an extended silence from both parties, Taylor is the first to speak her opinion on the matter. "Well, Mr.

Houston, I never thought it would be *you* they'd set me up with. I feel like an E-harmony match gone wrong."

Trent narrows his eyes. Gosh, I hope this doesn't get ugly. "Look, Taylor. I don't want to be here any more than you do. So just stop whining and maybe after a while they'll let us go."

I shake my head, ashamed of them both. I've got to be the one to end this faux feud they've got going on. "Taylor, Trent's crazy about you, and you've been drooling over him since he walked up. Shut up and enjoy your date with him, or you'll never get out of here." All three of them, including Lexie, raise their eyebrows at me like I've said I eloped with a camel, but I don't care.

Trent takes a seat in front of Taylor. "Is that true?"

Taylor's face grows redder by the second. "Well, maybe..." she mumbles.

Trent releases a sigh of relief. "Good, because what Riley said last semester while we were in science was true. I've liked you since the fifth grade."

Taylor glances down at the table, attempting to suppress a smile, though it's a lost cause. "Fine." She slaps her hand across the table, palm up for Trent. "Go ahead, hold my hand, you adorable idiot."

"Whoa, I didn't expect that!" Lexie laughs, shaking her head at me in bewilderment.

Can't Beat the Heart of a Carolina Girl

"Dang, we could run the E-harmony dude out of business," I ponder aloud.

Trent appears shocked at first, but the full-fledged grin that spreads across his face eases my worries. Lexie and I take this as a sign that our little scheme has worked, so we turn to go find my family's table.

Eyeing Trent as we're about to leave, I smirk. "Now we're even."

"Sure thing," he murmurs, reaching for Taylor's hand.

"Thank God that worked!" Lexie sighs as we turn the corner, reaching the section for larger seating.

"I know. Did you see the way he looked at her when she walked in? They're adorable!"

Lexie adjusts the hem of her blouse. "Yeah, it's perfect. Carter looks at you the same way. I mean, I know we're all still young and everything, but I'd love to have a guy look at me as if his whole world is standing in front of him, you know?"

I pat her shoulder, sympathizing easily. That's a feeling I haven't long forgotten. "Lex, don't feel bad. You'll find the right guy. He's out there somewhere waiting for you, too, but for whatever reason, it's not your time to meet yet. And I know it's cliché as crap, but they always say you only find love when you stop looking."

She shakes her head, ready to point out my flawed logic. "You decided you liked Carter about an hour or two after Brett rejected you."

"Well, you've got a point there," I admit, biting my lip to explain myself. "But I didn't develop feelings for Carter until I realized that he cares about me entirely too much for me to ignore him like Brett did me. Just the fact that it didn't take very long... well, Carter was already waiting there with open arms. Trust me, when God says your heart's ready, you'll meet him."

"Hey, Lexie!" Remy chimes as we join my family at their table. "What happened to Turkey Head Trent?" This is her infamous nickname for him, by the way.

"Let's just say he'll be preoccupied with a certain lady friend during lunch," I explain for Lexie, knowing that she's still musing over our conversation. The way she's biting her lip, I can tell that she's not going to shake this longing soon.

⌘

I enter Linwood Whaley High School the next Monday with an irreplaceable sense of pride. Whatever Hailey Carson feels like doing to me now is ignorant and superficial in its own way. Letting anything she conjures up affect me or my relationship with Carter will show mere disrespect to myself.

Can't Beat the Heart of a Carolina Girl

This morning I am taking on a new outlook: God has a purpose for everything and everyone, even me. He won't let me down.

Whilst taking my usual path to our morning meeting place, random people continue to gawk at me with odd expressions. In an attempt to push the thoughts aside, I say a little prayer in my head, keeping my chin up. The opinion they've formed of me is biased and disillusioned. Who cares what they think? All I'm sure of is that my friends, Brett, Carter, and I know the truth of the matter, and that's all that matters.

Upon meeting up with my friends, they immediately ask how I'm doing, as if I'm suffering from a fatal disease or something since the rumors have yet to subside. I sigh, rehashing the events from Friday to them for the first time. Inevitably, they're as disgusted with Hailey as I am.

"Are you serious?" Taylor spits in fury. "Riley, we can't just stand here and let her trash your reputation. You are so much better than what she's making you out to be. We've got to do something about this!"

I explain to them that revenge is not worth it because, in the end, Hailey will always get what she wants. Guys, revenge, domination. It doesn't matter to Hailey. If she wants it, she gets it. It's just a stupid fact of life.

"Well, that's no fun, but at least you're still with Carter, right?" Lexie says. I'm about to answer when Carter runs up to me, spinning me around in his arms. "Oh, well, I reckon so!" she laughs.

"Carter, what's going on?" I ask, catching my breath.

"You're never going to believe what happened!" Carter exclaims, revealing an enthusiastic grin. All three of us coax him for an answer.

"What happened?" I prod, shaking his shoulders.

Carter smirks at my impatience. "Brett turned in Hailey to the principal for repeatedly harassing an innocent student. You know, plus the other dozen or so she's got on her hit list. I heard that Principal Brown expelled her from school."

"You mean she's finally gone?!" My feet turn into springs beneath me, allowing me to bounce up at the joyful news. With Carter enveloping me in a tight embrace, I finally feel that all is right in the world, until I recall the loophole that is bound to occur. "Wait... won't her dad pay off Principal Brown to let her back in? I knew this was too good to be true."

Carter ruffles my hair. "No, that's the beauty of it. As soon as her parents found out about the whole thing, they came out here with a huge check trying to bribe him. Luckily, since Principal Brown is such a stickler for the rules, he turned them down. You're free from her grasp, Riley. We're all free!"

Though I fear that my lips are about to explode from smiling so much, the fact of the matter is that we still have to live with Hailey's aftermath. The rumor mill is still turning at full force. Hailey's finally being held accountable for her actions, yet the lies she and her gang have created will survive her absence. So I'm not really escaping anything, now am I?

The bell for first period rings, and my friends and I scatter our separate ways. I enter the gym with a bit more dignity, because without Hailey around I can stand to be a more confident person. As I head for the locker room, Nichole and Tiffany are scurrying around like beheaded chickens. I guess they're incapable of thought without their dictator around.

Setting my gym bag down on the changing bench, I unfold my shorts and T-shirt. The intercom buzzes as Principal Brown begins the morning announcements. For the most part, I couldn't care less if the varsity softball team made it to the state playoffs, or if the debate team is heading off to a regional competition in Myrtle Beach. What catches my attention is his last statement: "And now, a word from Brett Harvey."

"Hey everyone." Brett's voice echoes throughout the campus, drawing everyone's attention. "I know you've all heard about the incident that took place this morning involving freshman, Hailey Carson. Why did this happen, you may ask? We all know Hailey. Her name has been known throughout Linwood County since that fateful day in 1994 when her money-famed parents gave birth to their so-called 'diamond among stones'. She has embarrassed her peers countless times, and *this*, my fellow Linwood Whaley students, is not nearly a fraction of the pain and torment she has brought upon my dear friends Riley and Carter."

In my peripheral vision, I'm aware that girls around the locker room are gawking at me. Returning my attention to my gym bag, I refuse to look up.

"And what exactly did Miss Carson evoke on these innocent students? She created numerous lies circulating around the myth that Riley has been cheating on Carter, among other things. I know all of you have heard the rumors, or have seen the forwards she has sent out containing this false information. If any girl has cheated on their boyfriend here at Linwood Whaley High School, it has been Hailey herself. She has done far more than the wrongs she has accused Riley of, and based on her extensive history of harassing students, she has been expelled from our school.

"If anyone chooses to further humiliate Riley or Carter, or any other student for that matter, Principal Brown will make it his business to have the exact same consequences in store for you. Harassment is a crime, so don't do it. Great, now I sound like a cop! Anyway, have a great day, everyone!"

Laughter envelopes the room as Brett ends his announcement, and from that minute on, the rumors subside and apologies surface. People who have been giving me the cold shoulder admit that they were wrong to have allowed the rumors Hailey and her crew created to form a negative opinion of me. This all touches my heart, but I have a deed to do myself. Someone else deserves an apology, because I know how heartbreak feels and I can't force that upon a friend. I need to talk to Brett.

⌘

Amongst the noise and traffic the Monday dismissal bell arouses, I plunge down the towering staircase from Mr. Park's Geometry class, searching for the honest heart who has freed Carter and me from the brutal clutches of a high school drama story. As I reach the end of the first floor hallway, I see Brett walking out of the exit door and heading to the parking lot. Quickening my pace, I race after the dark-eyed miracle worker.

"Brett, wait!" I shout, becoming breathless as I jog closer to him. He turns around, his smile noticeably forced. My heart's crushed by the grave reflection in his eyes. Sometimes being the heartbreaker and knowing it is just as painful as being the one with a wounded heart.

"What do you want?" he asks, his eyes as wet and cold as they were the day he had heard the news of Hailey's affair.

Taking in a deep breath, I make an attempt to calm my nerves, though it doesn't help in the least. Instead, with my voice shaking and a harsh pain the back of my throat, I whisper, "Thank you so much, Brett."

194

"Oh, it was nothing," he replies, the bitter tone hitting me with full force as he continues to walk to his truck.

I grab his shoulder, forcing him to turn around. His mouth opens to fuss me out, but I give him a look of reassurance. "Brett, what you did this morning was not nothing. It was amazing. If it wasn't for you, all of those people would have continued to live in the expectation of the lies that Hailey created. Carter and I would have to suffer here at school for three more years from the results of a tainted reputation. Actually, without you, I'm pretty sure Carter and I would be over."

My mouth burns with distaste at my last statement. Regarding my reaction, Brett reveals a melancholic smile. "Well, that's just my luck, isn't it?"

"What do you mean?"

"If I had not helped you, you would probably be single now, which is what I wanted. It could've been my chance to make you mine." I stand dumbfounded, nodding simply because I don't know how else to respond. "But," he continues, running his hand over his face, "I chose to help you two out anyway. I know you and Carter love one another. I see it every time you guys are together. He only has eyes for you, Riley. I've never seen him so much as glance at another girl the same way he does you. That's why I did it. You may not like me that way anymore, but it's important to me that you be with the guy that cherishes the gift he has in you. I just hope that someday I can find someone to love like that."

Can't Beat the Heart of a Carolina Girl

Tears stream from both our eyes as I pull him in for a hug. "Don't worry. There's no doubt in my mind that you will someday. And thank you so much for talking with Carter the other night about our argument. Without you, I'm sure he'd still be hating my guts right now."

Brett pulls away for a second. "Wait, that little turd told you about that?" My appalled expression elicits a laugh from him. "What? He broke the most sacred rule in the guy handbook!"

"And what might that be?" I question, now curious.

"Guys are never, and I mean *never* supposed to tell their girlfriends about getting relationship advice! Especially if it's from the guy they had to win the girl over from. What was he thinking?"

I laugh to myself, shaking my head at his remarks. "He told me because he wanted me to know how sweet you were, since you're the one who got us back together, Mr. Love Connection." Brett smirks, shrugging the compliment off.

"Oh, and by the way, I made an A minus on my Geometry test. Thanks. I couldn't have done that without you, either," I state, pivoting to make my way back to the school.

"What can I say? I'm a man of many talents," he calls back. I roll my eyes at his craziness and stroll back to the front of the school where I meet Carter with a kiss. From this moment, I'm assured that everything is going to be fine.

196

Chapter Twenty

Eventually the glorious, long awaited day that kids of all ages enjoy emerges from the shadows… the last day of school! Like anyone else I'm ecstatic, yet a bit disappointed when I realize how quickly freshman year has passed. I guess it's true what all my older relatives have said about their high school years: they fly by as fast as the winds of a Carolina hurricane.

Today our only assignments are to joke around in class, ask our teachers what we scored on our final exams, and meet on the football field fourth period to get our friends to sign our yearbooks. I've just picked up my copy from the auditorium before heading out to the spacious green field, so I turn to the freshmen section to check out my picture.

"That Riley Houston chick's picture is pretty gorgeous," Carter compliments, taking a peek at the picture before I hide the book behind my back.

"No it's not!"

"Well, you must have not gotten a good look at it then," he responds, maneuvering the book away from my grasp.

Can't Beat the Heart of a Carolina Girl

"Riley Houston, page 131," he says after looking up the page number in the index. Carter scans the rows of students, locating my photo in the fourth row. "Beautiful." I shake my head in disagreement. "Well then, should I say alluring? Breathtaking? I don't know how else to describe it. It's certainly not ugly." Carter hands me the book, pointing at my picture. "Look, you stubborn thang."

As I peer down at my freshman yearbook photograph, I'm left speechless. Compared to my preceding school pictures, this one is the best by a long shot. No lack of confidence, no jungle-thick bangs, no robot teeth. All that my picture contains is the Riley Houston that has emerged from her cocoon and somehow managed to transform into a beautiful person.

"Okay, it's pretty good," I admit, rubbing the back of my neck.

Carter's expression is smug, yet still bears a hint of goober. "Told you. You're the most beautiful girl in this book Riles. At least to me." He takes my hand, kissing it. "And I'm beyond thankful that God allowed this year to happen."

"Aww!" Trent and Taylor bellow in unison as they walk up from behind us.

"Aww!" Carter and I retort back equally obnoxious, referring to the fact that they're holding hands.

"I told you that you two were meant to be together," Trent smiles. "Carter's never been 'romantic' until he met you."

"Neither have you, dude. Now that you and Taylor are together, all you talk about is how pretty she is, and how smart she is, and how funny she is. What happened to the fart jokes, Trent?"

Carter and I laugh as Trent's face turns a light shade of pink. Taylor kisses his cheek. "Maybe I like this Trent."

Trent smiles, obviously relieved. "Perfect."

"Hey bestest friend in the universe, can I sign your yearbook?" Lexie jumps on my back, almost giving me a heart attack.

"Please. If you don't kill me first, that is." I giggle, throwing her off.

"Me next!" Taylor runs to Lexie's side to see what she's writing.

"Hey Lex, can I write something in yours?" I ask. She passes me her copy of the Linwood Whaley High School's *Authoring Arrowheads*. I flip to the autograph pages and write:

Dear Lex,

I still can't believe that my best friend moved back to Grahamwood. It's going to be awesome now that we can spend the rest of our high school years hanging out just like old times. Thanks so much for putting up with all of my mess this year. You're the true definition of a best friend forever.

-Riley Houston

Can't Beat the Heart of a Carolina Girl

Handing Lexie's yearbook back to her, I wait for Taylor to finish before asking Carter to sign mine. Meanwhile, Carter's signing Trent's book while simultaneously making fun of Trent's face in his picture.

"I had gas, okay?" Trent snorts as he finishes signing Carter's yearbook.

Taylor hands my yearbook back to me, and I read over what my friends have written. A warm feeling overwhelms me when I take in their heartfelt comments. At last, I feel accepted in my little world.

"Riles, will you sign my yearbook now?" Carter requests, passing his yearbook to me. We exchange a smile as I give him my copy. Of course, Carter. You are my boyfriend, after all.

Dear Carter,

What can I say, other than that our freshman year together has been nothing but amazing. When we met on the first day of school, I secretly knew that I'd never forget that moment. I'm so glad that we finally got the courage to get to know each other. Sure, we've had our ups and downs, but like you told me before, nothing can alter God's plans. Carter, I love you, and I can't wait to spend the rest of our high school years as your girlfriend."

-Yours forever, Riley Houston

Allyson Kennedy

Am I doubtless thinking that Carter and I will spend the next three years together as a couple? Am I a hundred percent sure that this is God's plan for our lives? No one can assure that a high school romance will last forever. No one can assure that any love will last forever. However, in my fifteen years, I'm sure that I've never felt this way about a guy before. I know that Carter loves me just as I am. I'm sure that he'll put in an equal effort to make this love last. And, most importantly, there's no doubt in my mind that as long as I keep my sights set on God to lead me, no force will be able to beat the heart of this Carolina girl.

Acknowledgements

Foremost, a huge thank you is in order for my Heavenly Father for giving me the gift of writing and allowing me to publish my first novel. Though my faith has wavered throughout this process in terms of my abilities, you have remained by my side nonetheless, and I will forever seek to honor You in all of my future endeavors.

This novel would not be possible without two amazing women in my family: Grandma Joyce, and Aunt Sherry. Grandma Joyce has served as my constant source of inspiration whenever I feel as if this whole writing dream of mine will never pan out, as she also loved to write but never attempted to publish her works before she passed away in 2006. Her crazy laugh and sassmaster comments will forever remain in my memory, and I am proud to be deemed her "mini-me" by the rest of the family. Aunt Sherry, without that small nudge you gave me to write stories in that Mary-Kate and Ashley notebook you gave me for Christmas back in 2001, this novel would cease to exist. Thank you for giving my dream a head start!

And of course, where would I be without the rest of my family? Momma and Daddy, I am forever indebted to you for supporting this crazy dream of mine from the beginning, and for aiding me through my array of mixed feelings about the publication process. Mander, thank you for being the best little sister in the universe. No fear; Remy isn't based off you (minus the Scooby-Doo mention)! To all of my aunts, uncles, and cousins (because let's be honest, there's a bunch of y'all and the list would be longer than the entirety of this novel), thank you for always asking me about my writing and for reminding me that family bonds are a vital and lifelong relationship that will bring forth both comfort and joy for years to come!

Special shout-outs are in order for Lindsay Hemby and Hannah English, my best friends from high school who I relayed my hopes and dreams for *Can't Beat the Heart of a Carolina Girl* to years ago during our sophomore year. Thank you both for fangirling with me about the possibility of publishing a novel way back when. I'll never forget all of the laughs we've shared! In addition, a huge thank you is in order for my cousin Patty for reading the first draft of this novel back in 2012. Without your input, I wouldn't have had the guts to pursue publication. To my beta readers: Hannah, Faye, Aunt Brenda, Cassidy, Amanda, and Mander, thank you for helping me go over and make necessary changes before publication. Without your feedback, I'd be in a mess!

Lastly, I'd like to thank a special guy in my life that has proved to me that guys like Carter still exist. You've been my confidant throughout the publication process for this novel, never growing annoyed with me as I rehashed the difficulties I faced to you on a sometimes daily basis. Thank you for reminding me to have faith that God will see me through this opportunity if it's in His Will for me (Lord knows how much I needed to hear that!). Like Riley and Carter's story, I'm not sure what our future will hold, but I thank God every day for allowing us to meet one another.

About the Author

A native of eastern North Carolina, Allyson Kennedy fell in love with writing at age seven while filling the pages of her Mary-Kate and Ashley notebook. Dozens of notebooks later, Allyson has penned short stories, poems, song lyrics, and two novels. After the second of her three writing contest wins at the University of Mount Olive, God planted a seed in her heart to pursue self-publishing her debut novel, *Can't Beat the Heart of a Carolina Girl*. When she's not writing, Allyson enjoys reading, blogging on her website, Authoring Arrowheads, reviewing books and movies for indie Christian authors and filmmakers, and following God's plans for her life. Her next release, *Speak Your Mind*, is set to be published in November 2018.

If you enjoyed reading
Can't Beat the Heart of a Carolina Girl,
please consider leaving a review on
Amazon and Goodreads!

For more from Allyson Kennedy, you can find her online at:

Website:
https://authoringarrowheads.wordpress.com/

Facebook:
https://www.facebook.com/authoringarrowheads/

Twitter:
https://twitter.com/authoringarrows

Goodreads:
https://www.goodreads.com/author/show/16469483.Allyso
n_Kennedy